SHATTERED

By TP Hogan

National Library of Australia Cataloguing-in-Publication entry

Hogan, TP.
  Shattered / TP Hogan
  ISBN: 9780992587604 (paperback)
  For young adults.
  Love stories. Young adult fiction.
  Kopke, Frank M., editor.
  Pederick, Amanda, editor.
A823.4

Acknowledgements

With thanks to all those who gave me encouragement over the years, and those who answered my questions night and day, no matter what they were.
Leanne, Phil and Melissa in particular.

Special thanks to my husband for the immortal words *"Well write it."* and all his encouragement and assistance in wrestling the story with me edit after edit; despite my character, grammatical and spelling foibles…and the fact that he doesn't read romances.

Chapter One

Mattie skidded to a halt on the slick, muddy lane-way.

Through the pouring rain she could just make out the sign post. It might say Marshwood Lane. It was the fourth left so it should be Marshwood Lane. According to the directions her mum had e-mailed, she would find the Manor at the end of it... if it was the right one. It was slow going as she crept through the deluge.

With the tyres crunching slowly over the gravel driveway, Mattie gave a low whistle as the manor came into view. She knew that step-dad number five was well off; an Earl who owned a house that was a part of the National Trust 'Historic Open Houses' scheme. She had assumed that the title had been honorary, merely a title. Never in her wildest dreams had she even considered that Alex might live in a real castle. While it wasn't a fairy tale castle, the Manor possessed an architecture that was beautifully elaborate but sadly no longer built. It was impressive. Even through the rain she could see the grey cut stone and stunning arched windows.

The driveway fanned out, branching off at an elegant sign proclaiming public parking to the left and private to the right. Mattie could see the private lane curve around and continue beyond a closed set of elaborate wrought iron gates. The public lane led to a large gravel car park already half-filled with vehicles.

The e-mail said to enter the house via the side door; something about the curator letting her in to the living area of the estate. She hadn't said anything about parking. Reversing into an empty bay Mattie willed the downpour to ease. She only needed long enough for the dash to the house. After several minutes of continuing rain, she resigned herself to getting wet. She hadn't even thought to pack an umbrella. Umbrellas should be handed out at the airport on arrival anyway. After all, this was England. The freezing water made her gasp as she hurried toward the safety of the building.

The imposing front doors were easy to find, they were beneath the large sign that bid guests 'Welcome to Ashcombe Manor'. Hoping that 'private parking' also meant private entry, she took the path to the right of the house and found herself on a flagstone path beneath an archway of climbing roses. The foliage kept most of the rain at bay, allowing only the occasional fat drop through. Glad of the temporary reprieve, Mattie hunched into her jacket and stepped carefully on the flagstone pathway, hoping that her non-grip sneakers wouldn't slip, although she was already so wet that taking a fall into a puddle wouldn't make any difference. Thankfully, there was a small covered portico over what looked to be the side door. She knocked and tried slicking her wet hair from her face. After a brief moment, the door was opened by an extremely handsome man. His hazel eyes regarded her with interest.

"Yes?"

"G'day. I'm looking for Jonathan Ashcombe."

"You've found him. I gather from your accent you would be the sister with the strangely masculine name." His tone was dry as he looked her over without moving from the doorway.

"Guilty." She grinned.

His short reddish hair was made brighter by the grey and black jumper he wore and his face was strikingly well structured, rugged more than classically handsome. Her fingers itched to sketch him.

"You don't look anything like your mother."

"So I've been told. I take after me dad. Um, do you mind if I come in? It's bloody freezing out here."

She was used to the surprise at her appearance by now. Her mum was naturally blonde with a few added highlights as she'd gotten older, five foot three and slim as a pencil. Mattie was a mousy brunette, five foot eight and a rather curvy size fourteen bordering too closely to a size sixteen for her comfort.

"Yes, of course. Where are my manners? Come into the kitchen, it's warmer in here. You may make yourself a cup of tea while I have someone bring in your bags, and then you can change into some dry clothes."

"Thank you. I parked in the public car park, the blue sedan with a hire company written on it. Bugger, I can't remember what it's called."

"Never mind. I am sure Erickson will find it."

"Erickson?"

"Our butler."

"You have a butler?"

"And several maids, menservants, gardeners, cooks and a few stable hands. Oh, I almost forgot the chauffeur. So you see, only the necessities."

She shucked her arms grateful for the heating in the house. "And only the bare necessities at that."

"How old are you?" Jonathan asked suddenly.

"Twenty-eight. You?"

"Thirty-two, so that makes you my bratty little sister."

"And you apparently are the annoying big brother."

"I aim to please."

Mattie laughed. At least he had a sense of humour. She was afraid he would be one of those stuck up Poms with a snotty attitude. He led her to the kitchen and pointed out where to find everything for a cuppa, then disappeared, presumably to find "Erickson".

She made her tea and sat as close to the wood heater as possible, slowly defrosting. At least this was only a visit and she wouldn't have to try to acclimatise to this awful weather. The kitchen's façade was old fashioned but the fittings were surprisingly modern. It looked like it would be well suited to someone who loved to cook. Unfortunately that 'someone' wasn't her. Shifting closer to the heater she saw movement out of the corner of her eye. For some reason there was a huge mirror that covered the back of the old fire place. It had a fascinating frame. Intrigued, she got up to inspect it.

"There we are, all organised. If you wait a moment, the guest room will be ready and you may change clothes and bathe if you like."

"Sounds heavenly Jonathan. Thank you."

"Are all you Australians the same? The moment the weather gets slightly cool you seem to act as if you were stranded in the snow."

"Only those of us that live in the north. I'm sure if you asked a Tasmanian he would enjoy the weather."

"If you live in the north then you should be accustomed to the colder weather."

"The Land Down Under, remember? North is closest to the equator, it's warmer."

"Of course." Jonathan said obviously unconvinced. "Would you like a tour of the living area? I would offer you one of the Manor, but the last tour for the day began five minutes ago, besides the ghost tour is more fun."

"Okay. You have a ghost?"

"Ghost tour. On Thursday evenings a night tour is held, and yes it is said we have a ghost. If you listen to the tour guides they will tell you we have several."

"Meaning you don't actually have a ghost."

"I personally have never seen a ghost but I have seen things moved about for no apparent reason."

"Uh huh."

Mattie didn't believe in ghosts. Once you were dead you moved on in one way or another but you didn't stick around to haunt the living.

"You'll see, believe me. The telephone unplugs itself on a regular basis and items of furniture and other things move about when no one has moved them.

"You're having me on."

"No. It actually happens." He insisted.

A brief knock came at the door and a girl in a dark uniform stood in the doorway.

"Excuse me Master Jonathan, the guest room is prepared."

Mattie followed Jonathan through the house… living area… as he gave her the tour. Most of the rooms were cluttered with overstuffed furniture and an over-abundance of knick-knacks of all types and descriptions. The ground floor held a large study, the kitchen, dining room, large entertaining room, a sitting room, a conservatory, and a games room. The second floor had seven bedrooms, another sitting room, a huge library, a few bathrooms and a second sun room.

"The top floor acts as the family offices and archives. All very modern and clinical, I'm afraid. " Jonathan announced closing the sun room door.

"You are missing a laundry."

"It is not missing. Beneath the kitchen are the old servants quarters that have been revamped and now hold a large laundry and a rather impressive wine cellar, if I do say so myself. And this…" he said with a flourish. "…is your room."

Mattie let out a low whistle as she took in the décor of the room. It looked like it came from a movie set. It held the biggest and highest four poster bed she'd ever seen. She ran her hand over the elaborately carved dresser, and inspected the detail of the design around the large oval mirror. The indentations were so fine they tickled her fingertips. The wardrobe held the same design. While the room was large she could barely navigate her way through with two lounge suites; two arm chairs; a wrought iron table with matching chairs and various tables with all sorts of bits and pieces. Surely no one needed all this furniture.

"It's beautiful."

"Don't be too impressed. It's decorated with cast offs from the manor."

"It all adds to the charm."

"It is lucky for you the bathroom doesn't have the same charm. You will notice that we do provide a modern lavatory inclusive of running water. We even have hot water for your shower or bath, whichever you prefer."

Mattie laughed. "Much appreciated. Um, where are my bags and stuff."

"You'll find them in the top shelf of the wardrobe."

"I still have to unpack."

Jonathan opened the wardrobe doors. Her clothes where neatly hung, folded, stacked and sorted in their appropriate places.

"You will find your toiletries in the bathroom. Anything that needs washing or pressing simply leave in the basket by the door, I'll be in the games room when you are finished."

"Thank you."

"*No worries*." He said with a shrug managing to mangle her accent atrociously.

After Jonathan had left her to her own devices, she grabbed some dry clothes and headed for the shower. The bathroom was heated. Bliss. She grinned at the huge old fashioned clawed bathtub. That was definitely on her to-do-list, but not right now. Right now warm and dry took priority. As she undressed she scowled at her reflection. What was it with this place and all the bloody mirrors? It seemed like there was at least one in every room, and they were all so big. Perhaps it was to give the impression of space. Goodness knows with all the 'dust collectors' and over-abundance of furniture the impression of space was sorely needed.

Dropping her sodden clothes into the basket she made the shower as hot as possible and gratefully stepped under the steaming spray with a sigh. The hot water was wonderful and the pressure was glorious, unlike her pitiful excuse for a shower back home. When she felt human again she stepped out of the shower and laughed. Even in the short amount of time she'd been under the water she'd fogged up the entire bathroom. Clearing the mirror with the towel she froze.

There was a man behind her.

Whirling she spun to face him, holding the towel to her body.

She was alone.

The door was closed.

Slowly she faced her reflection again. She was the only one there.

"Jet lag." She told herself as she dried herself, her heart slowly returning to its normal pace. She'd been awake nearly nineteen hours and had crossed more than one time zone. It wasn't a wonder she was seeing things.

She nodded to herself as she reached for her clothes. "That's all it is. Jet lag."

Chapter Two

"Sit still."

"I *am* sitting still." Jonathan insisted even as he shifted in the armchair.

"Put your arm back."

"It's gone numb."

"You can move in a moment but until then, put your arm back."

With a sigh Jonathan placed his elbow back on the arm of the chair and rested his fingers at his temple where Mattie had posed him.

"You could have at least warned me of the slow torture."

"You said you would do it now stop being such a wuss."

"Such a what?"

"Wuss, sook, whinger. Lift your chin a little."

"I should have made it best out of five."

"Then you would have had to sit here for longer."

"I could have won."

"Not bloody likely. I won all three games."

"How did you get to be so good at ping pong anyway?"

"A mis-spent youth. There …" Mattie gave the page one last stroke. "… All done. You can move now."

"May I see?" He tossed the book on the carpet and leapt from the chair trying to peer over her shoulder.

Mattie pulled the sketch pad protectively against her chest.

"I said you could move, not gawk."

"Be fair. I have just sat as still as I have ever been, even Father would have been impressed. You have to give me some sort of prize for it."

"Let's see. What was it you said earlier when I told you you'd have to honour our bet? That's right… sod off." She recited meaningfully

"I still honoured the wager." He snatched the pad from her hands.

She tried to keep her grip on it and failed. Silently she watched him view the sketch with baited breath. Normally no one would see her sketches until she was completely satisfied and this was definitely not the case. Jonathan had been posed casually with one hand at his temple and the other lazily turning the pages of a book. Even though he'd been talking most of the time she'd tried to draw his mouth in a half smile as if he'd found the contents of the novel slightly amusing. The smile hadn't worked as she'd wanted and needed some work but it was too late now.

"Goodness! When you said you drew I didn't expect this! You could sell this."

"I doubt that." Mattie laughed self-consciously. "Half-finished drawings usually don't sell very well, and besides most people prefer paintings."

"I'm serious."

"So am I."

Standing Mattie took the sketch pad from Jonathan, closed it and began packing her pencils and tools away.

"I would buy it."

"Yes well I am getting the impression that you are a little vain."

"Well when you have the advantage of perfection… seriously I think it is very good."

"Thank you. Usually artwork of relaxed men doesn't sell very well so maybe I'll give it to you anyway."

"Why not?"

"Don't know. Relaxed and reclining woman, active and busy men... that's what sells. My theory is that women are beauty and beauty is at its best when it is peaceful and relaxed. Men are strength and that is best shown in movement and action, even if that movement is still, like a man standing on the prow of a ship with the wind blowing his hair and clothing."

"Is that some romantic fantasy?"

"Nope. It's a work I painted that sold for quite a bit actually."

"Have you sold many paintings?"

"Enough that I don't have to starve, but not enough for the lap of luxury."

A sudden chime stalled Jonathan's next question.

"That will be Tiffany." He announced with a grin.

"You have a door bell?"

"Yes."

"Well there you go. You learn something new every day." Mattie followed him from the sitting room. Even after a week here she hadn't realised there was a doorbell.

"Mattie this is Tiffany, Tiffany this is Mattie, my…"

"Really Jonathan you have dipped low this time. She really isn't your usual sort." Tiffany commented in a disdainful tone.

Mattie looked down at herself. Alright, so she had bought her current outfit entirely from second-hand stores. Still she must have made some sort of impression to have the other woman want to guard Jonathan as her own.

"I hadn't realised you had a usual sort when it came to step-sisters."

"Step-sisters?"

"Yes as I was about to say this is Mattie Day my new step-sister." Jonathan explained.

"Actually 'Day' is my other step-father's name. I'm Mattie Holmes and am I correct in assuming that you are Jonathan's girlfriend?"

"One of many. Jonathan is not an easy man to pin down." She gave him a lascivious wink.

"Darling, you could 'pin' me anytime."

"And don't I know it."

"Okay." Mattie said slowly and the other two laughed. "I'll leave you two alone."

"No stay. We had plans to watch one of Jonathan's thousands of flicks. You should join us."

"What are you going to watch?"

"I don't know yet, whatever takes my fancy."

"Yeah, why not? I've got nothing better to do. I'll just put this away." Mattie indicated the sketch book.

"Meet in the theatre."

Mattie grinned as she raced up the stairs. It was ages since she had taken the time to watch a movie just for the fun of it, and there was nothing better to do on a rainy afternoon. As she left her room again, Stacey came out from behind a panel across the hallway carrying a bottle of window cleaner and a roll of paper towel.

"Don't tell me this place has secret passages."

"No Miss, just servant ones."

In the two weeks she'd been here, Mattie had finally got Stacey to stop curtsying every time the maid saw her; although she hadn't quite stopped Stacey from calling her 'Miss'. It made Mattie feel like a school teacher.

"Where does this go?"

"To the kitchen."

"Cool. Can I use it?"

"I don't see no reason not to, it's just nobody but staff does."

Stacey showed her how to open the panel then returned to cleaning the glass. The panel opened to a landing with an elevator and the entrance to a set of stone stairs. Deciding on exploration rather than convenience Mattie took the stairs.

The steps were narrow and showed signs of wear with a shallow depression in the middle of each tread. The walls on either side were covered in faded tapestry carpet. She assumed it had something to do with keeping the stairwell warmer than bare stone. About halfway down the stairs the tapestries on the walls gave way to two huge mirrors from floor to ceiling. Beyond the mirrors the tapestry carpet continued but Mattie stopped to look at her reflections.

"To infinity and beyond." She joked as she turned towards the right hand wall and gave herself a wave. The reflected reflections gave an endlessly reflected wave in return and she laughed. Looking over her shoulder to see her reflection from behind she froze.

The man from her bathroom had returned.

She spun.

He wasn't on the stairs.

Slowly she looked at the mirror on the left side of the stairs. He was most definitely there. He wasn't doing anything, just standing there looking at her. Switching her gaze to the mirror on the right hand side of the stairs she didn't see him. He wasn't there. She looked from mirror to mirror a few times more just to be certain.

How could he be in one mirror and not the other?

Why wasn't he on the stairs?

Her heart pounded into overdrive as one answer came to her.

He was Jonathan's ghost.

She stared at him for a moment but he didn't move or do anything sinister. If anything he seemed as surprised to see her as she was to see him. He was dressed in an old fashioned dark suit with a jacket that fell past his knees. Underneath his jacket he wore a dark grey waistcoat with light grey pinstripes, and a silver cravat held with what looked like a diamond pin. A stiff white shirt collar peeked out above the cravat circling his neck, and she could just see a black ribbon holding his dark hair back from his face.

His square jaw was clean shaven, his lower lip was fuller than his upper, and his nose was straight without being perfect. His high cheekbones gave his eyes a slightly boyish curve and their green colour could put emeralds to shame. He could have been considered classically handsome except that his face was too masculine, almost too hard. There was a tiny scar that sat at the edge of his left eyebrow and the slight flaw to his nose worked well to give him the aura of danger. She doubted she could do him justice if she were to draw him, but how she wanted to.

To her great astonishment he suddenly grinned and gave an elaborate bow. She'd been involved in a theatre production of something-or-other a few years ago and had learnt to do a proper curtsy so she dipped into one now with her head slightly bowed. If the ghost was going to be polite she might as well return the compliment. When she came out of the curtsy he was staring at her with a stunned expression. Perhaps he hadn't seen a curtsy for a while.

"I know it wasn't that crash hot but you don't need to stare."

He mouthed something.

Mattie shook her head and shrugged. She couldn't hear him. He pointed at her, placed two fingers under his eyes then pointed at himself.

She knew nothing about sign language but she took it to mean… *Can you see me?*… and nodded.

He shook his head as he stepped up to the glass and placed his hand against it. She placed her hand against his.

Suddenly he disappeared.

She stepped back from the mirror but all she could see was her endless reflections. For a moment she waited to see if he would return but he didn't.

"Okay." She said to herself then laughed.

Here she was, the girl who didn't believe in ghosts, standing in the middle of a set of stone steps waiting at a mirror for a ghost to reappear. With a shake of her head she descended the rest of the way and came out in the kitchen scullery. With a last look behind herself she set off to find Jonathan and Tiffany. No one would believe her. She didn't even really believe it herself.

Chapter Three

"Thank you."

The money quickly disappeared into the slotted box as Jonathan welcomed the last of the booked guests on the special ghost tour.

"On this Halloween tour, I would like to welcome you and warn you that this traditional witching day often calls forth ghosts, spirits and memories that are only rarely seen. If you follow me we shall begin our "journey into history" from the garden."

With that Jonathan winked at Mattie and set off into the depths of the Manor. She had the distinct feeling that some of the 'ghosts, spirits and memories' they would see tonight would have a helping human hand. Usually the idea of going through a house to learn some old history, quickly forgotten, left her cold but she did have an ulterior motive for tonight. She hadn't seen the ghost since the afternoon on the stairs but her interest was piqued. Every time she'd been able to slip him into the conversation with Jonathan, he had said that she should go on the tour, so here she was listening to him explain what they should do were any of them to get lost and where the emergency exits were.

She reasoned that a ghost wouldn't haunt a place unless it had something to do with his life or death. Tonight she would find out who the ghost was, how he had died and what he was doing haunting Ashcombe Manor. She had scoured the library for all or any information on what she had seen. There seemed to be no mention of ghostly apparitions appearing in mirrors although there were several legendary hauntings throughout the manor over the last few centuries.

A lady in white who haunted the garden seems to have been connected to one Jemima Middleton who drowned after having been jilted by her betrothed in about 1870.

A presence often felt in the main entry staircase was thought to have been a butler named Hamilton, who hung himself from the banister after being caught helping himself to large chunks of the estate finances during the late 1890's.

The mystery of the mobile furniture in the manor was thought to be connected to young Emily Pankhurst, daughter of the early twentieth century coachman, who died tragically of pneumonia in 1912.

It was possible that the ghost she had seen was that of Hamilton the butler but somehow she didn't think so. For one thing the description in the handbook said that he had a large elaborate moustache and the man she'd seen had been clean shaven.

Jonathan was quite knowledgeable and a charming tour guide. Unsurprising really; he had grown up with this history and it was his own family. Mattie found the start of the tour extremely ho-hum until Jonathan took them down a hallway which was lined on both sides with portraits and began to explain who they were and where they fit into the Ashcombe family tree. On one side of the hallway hung the portraits of first born Ashcombe men, while portraits of their wives hung opposite.

As Jonathan gave a short spiel at each portrait Mattie made notes of any Ashcombe that had died tragically or suddenly. She paused at each one and studied it carefully for someone who could be her ghost. None of the portraits looked exactly like the man in the mirror. None had a scar at his eyebrow and only a handful of them had the dark hair and green eye combination but by the end of the hallway she'd narrowed it down to five possibilities. Only two had hair and eyes the correct colour but she didn't want to dismiss the other three on that basis alone. There was such a thing as artistic license after all.

With only one exception, all had disappeared suddenly and without a trace. Walter Ashcombe disappeared in 1553, William Ashcombe disappeared in 1647, Eugene Ashcombe was murdered by his sister-in-law in 1715, Leonard Ashcombe disappeared in 1781 and Sebastian Ashcombe disappeared in 1869.

Jonathan led them to a dining room with a long table which was set to accommodate them all, lit only by candles. A row of servants in period costumes lined the walls and she recognised Stacey and several others among them.

"Now as we take an interval to our tour, please take a seat and your meal will be served." Jonathan said dramatically. The group which had been silently listening to the tour suddenly began to chat and laugh like school children let out from an exam.

"What is your accent dear? I noticed it when you asked a question at the portraits."

Mattie jumped as she was addressed by a small, elderly lady.

"Australian."

"There you go Fred, I told you she didn't speak English." She spoke to an older man about Mattie's height with a white brush of a moustache.

"Yes you did Elise."

Fred gave Mattie a quick apologetic smile and she could see the twinkle in his eye. She returned his smile. It was obvious he loved his wife despite her abrupt manner.

"What brings you to England?" Elise asked.

"Family."

"It's good to visit family. Our daughter is visiting at the moment with her children. They are such beautiful girls. She doesn't like old houses though; it's not her 'thing'."

"How long have you two been married?" Mattie interrupted before the woman could launch into a long monologue about old houses.

"Forty-nine years tomorrow." Elise announced threading her fingers through Fred's who smiled indulgently.

"That's fantastic. Congratulations."

Mattie meant it. Coming from a family with so many divorces a long marriage was a rare feat indeed.

"Shall we sit?" Elise asked and Fred held out her chair.

Mattie smiled at the old fashioned chivalry. She'd never had a man pull out a chair for her.

"Mr Ashcombe I was wondering if you would tell me something that has struck me as curious. Why are there so many mirrors in the Manor?" Elise asked up the table as the servants set down the entrees.

"It is an Ashcombe tradition that started with Ernest Ashcombe. As a wedding present he gave his bride Natalia a large wall mirror. It is said that any Ashcombe descendent not to give a mirror as a wedding present will fall under the Ashcombe curse."

Jonathan had everyone's attention.

"What curse is that?" Elise asked.

"A man whose vanity was his lure. A love whose beauty is most pure. A heart must shatter on the inner. A single breath must pass the mirror."

"Charming. What does it mean?"

"I have no idea." Jonathan admitted easily with a grin.

Another guest claimed his attention with a question and Mattie frantically scribbled the words of the curse. It sounded like a badly made up rhyme.

The meal was superb and the conversation interesting but the rest of the tour was a waste of time. There was nothing more to be learned that could help her identify the mysterious ghost. After the last of the visitors left she anticipated a talk with Jonathan to hopefully pick his brain and get to the bottom of the mystery or at least give her a clue as to which lead to follow. He foiled her plan by grabbing the car keys and telling her he was going out with Tiffany and her friend Bethany and not to wait up.

Standing in the foyer for a moment she thought about her next step. She didn't want to give it up for the night just yet. Racing to her room she grabbed her sketch book and pencils and went into the hallway with the portraits. It was easier to draw subjects that held still and she wasn't aiming for master pieces. After about an hour she had copies of her five candidates that she was happy with and took them all to her room. Mattie cleared the largest table available, set up her laptop, spread out the books, notes, sketches, and other research she had collected over the past few days and began to tackle the arduous task of copying any references she found to her five suspect Ashcombes.

Despite the modern upgrades to the living quarters of the Manor, there was no photocopier, and she dare not take the books out of the house in case she ruined them somehow. It suddenly occurred to her that there might be one in the office on the third floor but it was too late now and she didn't want to wait until the morning. It reminded her of the research she'd done at school except the topic was history. She hated history.

Most of her friends found this fact amusing considering her mother was a manuscript restorer and historian. The books were so dry that she was in danger of nodding off, so she alternated between the tomes and the internet. After a few hours she found a description of Eugene Ashcombe and eliminated him from her list. He was described as having brown eyes like his portrait. It left four possibles, and each from a different century.

Her notes on three of them were quite extensive and she was leaning towards William Ashcombe as the most likely identity for her ghost. It was more of a hope then a true conclusion though. He was one of the two with green eyes and, admittedly, that was her only lead. She really needed some way to date her candidate. At least if she could figure out which century he came from then she would know who he was. Reaching across to the couch for the notebook she'd taken with her on the tour she saw movement out of the corner of her eye and turned towards the dresser mirror.

He was there.

"G'day." She waved after getting over the initial shock of his sudden appearance.

He lifted his hand in reply. Tilting his head in an exaggerated curious gesture he made a circle with downward palm then mimed reading. Mattie found the tome with the family tree and its history and carried it over to the mirror showing him the title. She then pointed at him before pointing at the book. He pointed at himself then at the book and nodded. Mattie couldn't stop the rise of excitement. If she understood him correctly, he was in the book and a member of the Ashcombe family.

It meant that Hamilton the butler was definitely out, but which Ashcombe was he? How the devil did she ask him? She sucked at charades and concepts were the hardest. She'd just have to start big and whittle her way down… twenty questions was going to expand to the 'n'th degree and then some. Going back to the disaster of research papers on the table and couch, she reached for the handbook Jonathan had given her at the beginning of the tour then stopped as a realization slowly dawned on her.

He could read.

She wasn't questioning his education or ability; it was only that the answer was suddenly so simple. Unearthing a blank exercise book from the pile on the table she grabbed a pen and sat down at the dresser.

Who are you?

Turning the book around she held it up at the mirror for him to read. She watched his eyes move as he read the words and his face lit up in a smile that made her breath catch in her throat. He was gorgeous. It was a good thing he was a ghost because a man who looked like that would never have dreamed of speaking with her if he was alive. She wasn't that lucky.

He sat down at the reflected dresser and her reflection went behind him. That was the best way she could describe it. It was as if he actually sat between her and her reflection, but that wasn't even the most disconcerting thing. His hand took hold of the reflection of the exercise book and the pen and moved them. They were no longer reflected in the mirror but an individual part of his 'world'. She almost expected her book and pen to move as his did but they didn't. By pretending that they sat opposite each other rather than a mirror she managed not to feel so weird, but it was still strange. For a moment he inspected the pen then, with it in his hand, mimed dipping it into something that wasn't there. At first she was confused then she realised he was expecting an inkwell.

The ink is in the pen, you just need to write.

She held up the exercise book again and he read it with a surprised look then nodded. Biting her lip she almost stopped breathing as he wrote in 'his' exercise book then he simply looked at her. Mattie tapped the mirror at the book to remind him to let her see. He smiled and shook his head, pointing at her book. Looking down at her open page her mouth dropped in shock. Underneath her writing his words had appeared in beautiful flowing script. The only problem was… she couldn't read it. It wasn't English. Her shoulders dropped in disappointment and she stared at the words. She hadn't thought of that. Frowning she looked at the words again. The letters were almost English, she recognised an 'A' and… suddenly she laughed.

Of course, why wouldn't it?

Since her book was no longer reflected in the mirror she grabbed the compact from her make-up kit and held it at an angle to the page. Now she could read it. The writing was mirror-reverse.

I am Mr Sebastian Ashcombe, at your service my lady.

He was one of her candidates. Of course he would have to be the one she couldn't find much information on. As she watched more letters appeared on the page as if by magic. She glanced up and saw him writing.

Whom do I have the honour of addressing?

My name is Mattie Holmes.

An unusual name for a lady. I have only heard of such a name in use as an abbreviation for Matthew. Surely that could not be your name.

It's short for Matilda. When I was younger people would tease me about being 'Waltzing Matilda' so I decided Mattie was easier.

Are you fond of dancing?

Mattie laughed. She was so used to people automatically making the connection that she hadn't even thought that he would misunderstand her.

Not particularly. 'Waltzing Matilda' is the title of a song back home.

Where is 'home'?

Australia. Do you know where that is?

Yes. The father of a childhood friend set sail to Australia with his family in Eighteen Fifty-three for the gold fields. It was said that you could pluck large nuggets from the ground with the ease and abundance of apples.

I doubt that was true. From what I can remember of my history lessons, gold digging was often long, hard, unfulfilling and profitless. Most of the gold was found in quartz veins that were hidden deep underground and not easily 'plucked'.

Of that I have no doubt. Nothing worthwhile is ever easily won.

I'm visiting my mother. Why did you call me 'My Lady'?

I do not wish to offend by presuming your marital status. As I can see no wedding band on your hand my first conclusion is to address you as Miss Holmes, however not wishing to imply that an attractive lady such as yourself would not obtain a husband I hesitate at such an address and thus resolve my dilemma by addressing you as My Lady.

Mattie reread his little spiel with a shake of her head. It was certainly original. Had it come from any man in her time, obviously worded a little less formally, it would have sounded like a brilliant 'come on'. Since he had disappeared in 1869 it was easier to accept that he truly did not 'wish to offend'.

Mattie is fine.

A small frown crossed his face and he looked surprised.

As you wish. However as you appear to have no objections to the intimacy implied by the use of a Christian name, perhaps you will also have no objections should I address you as Matilda. I have no desire to provide you with cause for embarrassment, if the use of your full name does indeed cause you such; I am simply uncomfortable with the use of such a masculine name for a lady.

It was Mattie's turn to frown. No one had asked to call her by her first name before. Everyone had just accepted the shorter version.

If it is as I suspect and there are very few who address you as Matilda you may return the favour and address me as Bastian. My mother was the only person to do so.

Mattie smiled. Bastian made him sound more approachable, less of a mystery and more human. Even if he was dead he could still be human.

Okay, Matilda it is. Can I ask you a question?

You have just done so.

How did you die?

Suddenly a great clattering came from the hallway followed by two girls giggling. Rising from the dresser she went to investigate.

"Shh. You'll wake Mattie." She heard Jonathan whisper as she opened her door slightly then quickly pulled it to.

"Oh tosh. If she wakes up she can just join us." A girl giggled in a loud whisper.

"Don't be crude Bethany. She's his step-sister."

Mattie recognised Tiffany's voice as someone landed heavily against the wall.

"They don't share blood. It wouldn't be incest."

"Behave yourself Beth." Jonathan admonished but by the sound of it he had other things on his mind.

"Do you *really* want me to?"

His door closed with a bang and the hallway was silent once more. Turning the handle of her door, she closed it tightly, glad his room was at the other end of the hall or she would have been in for a long night.

Looking at the mirror again she was disappointed to see that Bastian was gone. A glance at the clock told her it was almost three in the morning and with a sigh she picked up the exercise book from the dresser. It was almost strange to see its reflection. As she was about to close it she saw the final words Bastian had written. Even mirror-reversed she could read them clearly.

I didn't.

Chapter Four

That infernal noise was going to send him mad.

One of the things he hated most in this living prison was the distortion of sound. After nearly one hundred and fifty years he had hoped he would, at the very least, have become accustomed to it. Voices and other low sounds were muffled and vague as if from a distance or, perhaps more appropriately, as if through impenetrable glass. High pitched sounds were also muffled but were, at the same time, intensified. Over the years the sound from that idiotic thing had changed, and not for the better. Now, there were six of the beastly things throughout the house and it seemed everyone carried another with them. As the noise continued he cursed Mr Alexander Graham Bell and hoped the gentleman was roasting in hell.

Suddenly the shrill tone halted in mid ring and he gave a sigh of relief.

Blessed silence.

Looking out into the solid Manor, he scowled in annoyance. He had not seen Matilda leave the house, yet he couldn't find her anywhere and he had searched the entire building four times. It had been so long since someone had been able to see him; seventy years at least. He could not remember her name. They had spent years communicating through mime and he had never thought to put pen to paper. It was really such a simple idea and its brilliance was in its simplicity.

More out of boredom than curiosity he followed the maid who carried the handpiece through the house. The maid had reacted as if she'd caught sight of him several times but she never appeared to see him when he stood directly before her. She had started working at the Manor the year Gordon died so that would be ten years ago. She, he thought her name to be Maisy or at least something similar, knocked on Matilda's door and after a short pause entered the room. With a frown he moved to the mirror at the dresser just as the maid passed Matilda the telephone.

She had been sitting on the floor in front of the sofa but she'd faced it towards the fire place and he hadn't seen her. He watched her stand and tuck her hair behind her ear as she spoke into the grey handpiece. She wasn't the most beautiful woman he had ever seen, in fact she could be described as quite plain, but there was a genuineness about her that saved her from the label. He never understood the penchant that woman seemed to have during the last ninety years or so to wear their hair short. A woman's hair was her glory and it should tempt a man to release it all in a cascading mass down her back.

Matilda's brown hair was cut bluntly just below her shoulders and she usually wore it tangled about a collection of clips and combs but at the moment it was loose. Despite the lack of length he liked it out. She had deep brown eyes framed with long dark lashes topped by fine dark eyebrows. Her nose was straight and ended with a rounded tip above a nicely shaped mouth which had the slightest dent in the middle of the bottom lip but otherwise was quite ordinary. She was taller than most women, coming up to Jonathan's chin, so he judged her to be about five foot seven or eight and he liked the fact that she had curves. The women Jonathan seemed to prefer were all horribly skinny and in dire need of a good feeding.

Matilda was wearing tight greyish-blue trousers with a light purple butterfly trailing shiny flecks down the side of the left leg. By now he'd become accustomed to her peculiar habit of wearing several shirts atop one another, and today appeared to be no exception. The long sleeves of a navy blue top peeked out from under the shorter sleeves of a white shirt, over which she'd placed a tiny silver singlet; although why she would wear one over her shirts he couldn't even begin to fathom. Matilda took the telephone away from her ear, pressed it and turned around as if to give it to the maid. He could have told her Maisy had left the room soon after handing over the hand piece. She shrugged and placed it on the nearest table before sinking back out of sight in front of the sofa.

Bastian crossed his arms. That was no good, she hadn't noticed him.

Moving to the mirror in the bathroom he was glad to see she had left the door open. He saw half of her, through the open doorway, as she sat cross legged, and surrounded by loose leaves of paper, several books and that black 'L' shaped thing with the blue wash of light. She was leaning forward reading something and he waved trying to capture her attention. Without looking up she merely picked up another book with and frowned in concentration.

Not for the first time he wished someone could hear him when he spoke or at the very least when he tapped on the glass. How the devil was he supposed to have a chance in breaking the curse when people rarely saw him and then when they did he couldn't communicate proficiently? With a frustrated sigh he let himself fade from the mirror. It was clear she was not going to notice him anytime soon.

Changing his mind he emerged in the dresser mirror and saw that she had the writing book open beside that interesting pen. Concentrating hard he solidified the reflection on his side of the mirror. As long as he touched the item he'd solidified he could use it. The moment he released it, it would become a mere reflection once more. Ignoring the thudding headache that always accompanied the effort he sat at the dresser to write and noticed she had penned some things of her own.

> If you didn't die, how are you in the mirror?
>
> The Ashcombe family curse, it has something to do with the curse, right? Do you know what the rhyme means?

Bastian's eyebrows rose. When had it become the 'Ashcombe family curse'? As far as he knew he was the only one it affected. Laughing humourlessly he closed his eyes briefly and shook his head.

"Believe me, Mr Ashcombe you will have time to reflect upon your actions… in abundance."

If he'd known she had meant it literally his amusement and witty retort would have died before they were uttered. He couldn't even remember now what he had said but it had incensed her fury and he was still paying the price.

How do I get your attention when I
want to talk to you?

He blinked as the words appeared on what had
been a blank line and looked up to see Matilda
smiling at him. Her smile really did transform her
face. She was almost stunning.

You have just done so.

But you're here to read it. How do I let
you know I want to talk to you when
you're disappeared?

*Your grammar is atrocious Miss Matilda
and good morning to yourself as well. In
answer to your question, I have no idea.*

~~Bug~~ Drat

He smiled at her sentiment and wondered
what she had been about to write before her change of
mind.

I was hoping you could tell me more
about the curse.

Jonathan indicated that the curse
began in 1530 with Ernest Ashcombe
but I couldn't find anything mentioned
about it before 1870. In her diaries,
Dallas Ashcombe mentioned she went
into your room and swears she saw you
in the mirror, but there is no mention of
the rhyme so how does that fit in? Does
the rhyme explain how you got trapped
or is it explaining how you get out? It
has to be how you got in, right?
Otherwise you wouldn't be here, there

wherever. Can you tell me what it
means?

What rhyme would that be?

Matilda looked stunned and she stared at him
for a moment.

You don't know? I didn't even think of
that.

A man whose vanity was his lure.

A love whose beauty is most pure.

A heart must shatter on the inner.

A single breath must pass the mirror

Bastian read it several times trying to shake
the feeling that he knew it but it wasn't quite right.
Drawing his breath in through his teeth he suddenly
knew it.

Ashcombe man thy vanity keep thee

Till Love shines Beauty and in purity

Till shattered heart within pierce free

And with single breath, mirror pass'ed be

It had been the last clear thing he had ever
heard.

A little more poetic I'll give you that. I
thought you said you didn't know the
rhyme.

*It is not merely a rhyme Miss Matilda, it is
the curse. It is that which placed me in my
predicament.*

How did you get into the mirror?

You make it sound as though I had the choice, as if I were able to come and go at whim.

Bastian paused. He wasn't certain if even he understood how it had come to be, so how was he to explain to another?

I angered the wrong person. I remember hearing the words of the curse and a sudden blinding white light before finding myself as you see me, trapped behind the mirrors of the Manor.

Who did you anger?

He hesitated. This line of questioning could potentially lead down a path of his past not suitable for feminine ears.

The nurse of my betrothed was rumoured to be Gypsy and I failed to heed the accompanying rumours that she had powers alien to a Christian upbringing.

That would explain how you are still alive. The scarce information I could find on you says you disappeared in 1869, almost 150 years ago.

What information did you manage to find about me?

Unfortunately not a lot. Four lines.

Disappointed he waited for more but she didn't write anything.

You have my attention.

Hesitating she bit her lip, a small furrow appearing between her brows as she looked at him.

He waited. Finally she nodded slightly then began to write.

> Your birthday is February 28; you were apparently a womaniser, had an alleged mistress, no children, disappeared on your wedding day and were thirty-three at the time.
>
> *I find it somewhat disappointing that I should be summed up in such a small and dismissive way. As you can see there is clearly more to me than that which you have written.*
>
> That's all I could find. You were only mentioned in one book. I've been all through the library and I've spoken to the curator of the Manor and Jonathan, they had nothing more than what I've found.

He was flabbergasted. She had to have found more than that.

> *Surely there must be something more. A mention of the fine parties I hosted perhaps, and what of the doctor whom I funded in his research? I was Patron to the Dunmore Opera House; surely there is mention of that? Have the powers that be so forgotten me that I am nothing more than a mere by-line in a long forgotten account?*

Her reply was to rummage once more in the disaster of papers and books on the floor and produce 'The Ashcombe Family Tree and History'.

Concentrating he solidified the reflection enough to grasp his own copy of the book.

Which page?

1074.

He flipped through the large tome to the prescribed page. There was a paragraph on each Ashcombe man and he smiled as he saw his father's name. Beneath him was a paragraph on his brother, and beneath that, one on his nephew Matthew. He scanned the entire page but couldn't see his name. He looked at Matilda with a questioning look. She held up her book and pointed halfway through his father's paragraph and running it down to the end of Percival's. With a frown he began to read.

> *…which can still be seen. Benjamin sired five children to his wife Avril, two of whom were sons. Sebastian born February 28th, 1836 and Percival born April 19th, 1840. Benjamin died February 29th, 1876*

> *Percival Ashcombe is the only known second born Ashcombe to have carried on the Ashcombe name. He came unprepared to the task having only the misfortune of his elder brother to thank for the honour. A known womaniser, the rightful heir, Sebastian Ashcombe had shouldered the cloak of responsibility and shunned his bachelor ways to marry Miss Penelope*

Cranston, as per the wishes of his family, only to disappear on the afternoon of his wedding day. Some say he rejected his duty and eloped with a Miss Swann, said to be his mistress. Others claimed that he had fallen foul of the Ashcombe curse. Percival sired twelve children to his wife Dallas, with seven surviving, three of whom were sons. Matthew born April 17th, 1870, Christian born October Twentieth 1871 and Jeremiah (Jeremy) born July 30th, 1872. Percival died August 6th, 1903.

Matthew Ashcombe …

Sebastian sank disbelieving into the back of the dresser chair, his disappointment was devastating. Never in his wildest dreams had he thought that nobody would even want to remember him. His sudden understanding of the world and his infinitesimal part in affecting it made him feel very small indeed. The curse suddenly seemed less a tedious joke and far more like a true punishment. The reflection of the 'solid' Manor grew dark as he allowed his image to fade from the mirror. For the first time since entering this prison he wanted to be alone. How did one come to terms with a complete dismissal, not only as a family member but also as a human being? His entire existence had been all but ignored.

Chapter Five

"What are you drawing?"

"I'm not." Mattie answered Jonathan absently without looking up from the pieces of the Tangram puzzle in front of her.

"That's unusual." He commented as he sat down opposite and pushed a mug in her direction, sipping from his own as he did so.

"Thanks."

"You are most welcome."

He reached across the table and picked up the booklet with the shadow shapes and flicked through it before setting it back by her elbow.

"I can't make the soldier. I've tried but I simply can't do it."

"The soldier was easy. I found the bee hardest so far."

"There's a bee?"

"Yeah. Page seven."

"What are you doing now?"

"Attempting a candelabra."

"A candelabrum."

"Huh?"

"Candelabra is plural, candelabrum is single."

"Candlestick." She amended.

"Any luck?"

"Not really." With a sigh Mattie scooped the pieces into her hand then returned them to their wooden box. Her concentration was now shattered by Jonathan with his many questions.

"Do you want to play a game of poker?"

"Didn't you win enough hands last night?"

"Just enough. You should have stayed longer."

"Nah. With the amount of hands I was losing I would have ended up a legless heap. I really don't drink that much anyway."

"I don't doubt it. After you left the game moved from 'drink poker' to 'strip poker'."

"Then I'm glad I left. Even though I undoubtedly had more layers of clothing on than the other girls, the way I was losing it wouldn't have made all that much difference."

Not to mention that the idea of parading around naked, or nearly naked, in front of complete strangers was not a comfortable one. She'd done it before while she did her stint in amateur theatre and had to change costumes in a unisex dressing room, but the sexual innuendos had been flying thick and fast between Jonathan, Tiffany, Bethany and Helen, another of Tiffany's friends, as it was and that was with only the drinks. She didn't want to even think about the upped ante as the clothes had fallen.

"What time did you end up going to bed?"

"About three."

"You would have had your eight hours of sleep." Mattie held her mug between two hands. Jonathan had been yawning all morning. It was now four in the afternoon and he'd apparently had enough coffee.

"I said I went to bed at three, I didn't say I'd gone to sleep." He grinned with a wink.

"Ugh. Spare me the details. I really do not want to know."

"Do you like doing it?"

"Excuse me." Mattie stared at him hoping he hadn't just asked what she thought he had.

"The… puzzle. Do you like working it out?"

She gave a mental sigh of relief. "Yes. I like to think that I'm actually good at puzzles."

Jonathan suddenly stood and rummaged through the cupboard under the large CD collection. He returned to the table with a large mahogany box.

"Then you may have this. It's a puzzle box. My mother gave it me when I was seven and I have never been able to open it."

"Are you sure you want to give me something your mother gave you?"

"Yes. I'm never going to solve it."

"This may be a silly question but what is the puzzle box for? Just a game?"

"No." He tipped the box to show her a little drawer flush with the side of the box. There was one on each side. "Once you solve the puzzle you'll be able to open all four."

"What sort of things did you hide in this?"

"Nothing. As I said, I've never solved it. Mother said she found it in one of the cupboards in the Manor so it may have something in it, but I doubt it."

"And if I find anything?" She asked with a grin.

"You may keep it."

"Really?" She hadn't expected that answer. "Even if I find diamonds?"

"If you find diamonds, I shall have to consider it very carefully, but anything else is yours."

"Thank you."

"Don't mention it."

Mattie ran her hands over the paler pieces of wood set into the box that made the puzzle. It reminded her of the little plastic puzzle with the plastic squares with bits of picture on it that moved around to create a full picture. The only difference being that pieces of wood covered the top with no piece missing and there was no picture.

"What do I need to do to solve it?"

"I don't really know. Mother said it was similar to the puzzle you were doing, so my guess is you need to make the shape of something with the pieces, of what though, I have no idea."

"You don't have to make it too easy for me."

Jonathan returned her smile then raised his mug for a mouthful.

"That phone call from your mother the other day, did she tell you the new flight details?"

"Nope. Just that they'd extended their honeymoon and they'd get back to us with the details once they'd decided on them."

"How does that change your plans?"

"Doesn't really." Mattie took a mouthful of her own coffee and pulled a face. As usual, whenever other people made it for her, it didn't have enough milk. "As long as they return before New Year."

"Knowing my father they will be pushing that deadline."

"What's your dad like?"

"Well he looks like the portrait in hallway at the Manor and there are loads of photos around if you would like to see them."

"I didn't ask what he looked like. Mum already sent me photos. I'm more interested in what he is actually like."

"He was hardly around when I was growing up, and then after mother died he was around more but he was so strict. Looking back now it was because he suddenly found himself as a single parent with no idea what to do, but it was hell for me at school. I found myself banned from going to my friends' houses after school unless he'd met both the parents. Any after-school activity he would have a meeting with coach or teacher and find out what was needed, how many games or lessons, how much I would need to practice and then he would make sure I did it. Believe me I started only doing things I really enjoyed after that."

He laughed running his finger down the handle of his mug.

"I recall once when I was sixteen some children were having a party and I told him it was a party for winning a soccer game, which was a lie. One young lad, Aaron Moody I think his name was, held the party because his parents were out of town. In the middle of the party Father came storming into Aaron's house and ordered me out. I was mortified. Apparently he'd rung up the soccer coach to find out when the party was supposed to end. The coach naturally didn't know a thing about it. He went up to my room and saw my diary that I had left out on my desk with the address. He made me wash dishes, do the laundry and mow the lawn for a month while I was grounded."

"Serves you right. Had you actually done housework before that?"

"No. Mowing the lawn wasn't so bad. But you can't tell me you never did anything stupid like that when you were at school."

"Actually I can."

"What! Don't tell me you were a 'goody-two shoes'?"

"Nope, with my mother I didn't have to be. Usually Mum and I would organise the parties at our place then Mum would take everyone's car keys and disappear upstairs. We had a huge garage that Mum had made into a studio for me. Most people would crash in there with borrowed sleeping bags until they were deemed sober enough to drive."

"How did you deal with gate crashers?"

"We never had to. Only those with invitations were allowed in. It also helps when your Uncle and Grandfather are cops and one or both were able to give us a hand if things got too rowdy."

"That would have made you popular."

"I was never that popular to begin with, being an arty type, so it didn't bother me."

"So your parties were never very big?"

"The largest we had would have been about twenty-five people, but I think we've gone off the topic."

Just then the telephone rang and Jonathan reached across to answer it. By the sounds of things it wasn't going to be a quick call. Mattie shrugged and, giving him some privacy, took the puzzle box upstairs to her room.

Bastian was back.

After his sudden disappearance the other day she'd been looking for him in every mirror she'd passed. She had started to wonder if he was gone for good. He didn't notice her entry into the room. He was standing next to the reflection of the large table reading. Her glance flicked to the table on her side of the mirror and she realised he was looking at her sketch book.

"Hey."

Bastian didn't look up.

Mattie walked up to the dresser and knocked on the mirror. She didn't know if he heard her or merely saw her but he looked up with a smile. Grabbing the pen she wrote furiously.

> You didn't ask to look at that. Close it now!

Still holding the sketch book he crossed to the dresser and read what she'd written. His smile disappeared and he dropped the book. She expected it to fall on the floor but to her shock the book was suddenly part of the reflection again, closed on the table.

I humbly beg your pardon Matilda I did not mean to pry. I thought it to be part of your research material and only now picked it up. Forgive me.

You're forgiven. I'm sorry I snapped at you. I don't like people looking at anything I haven't finished and I over reacted.

Your reaction is as expected when privacy has been breached. I would not like a stranger to look through my things.

Would you like to see one that is finished?

Please.

Mattie collected the sketch book and flipped through to a drawing of Bastian she'd done from memory. Comparing the drawing against him she was satisfied that she'd produced a good likeness. Turning the book around, she showed it to him and watched his reaction. It wasn't what she expected. When people see themselves in a drawn picture there would be a flash of recognition and they usually smiled as their eyes searched the page. Bastian showed no sign of recognition.

You are quite talented. The detail in this drawing is extraordinary.

You don't think it's a good likeness?

He looked up at her with a confused expression.

It's supposed to be a drawing of you. I thought the likeness was good myself, but if you don't recognise yourself perhaps I should scrap it and start again.

NO. Please do not 'scrap' it. May I?

May you?

Take a closer look.

Mattie held up the sketch again. Bastian closed his eyes and after a moment took the reflection of the book into his hands. He looked at it for a long time and Mattie waited. Finally he picked up the pen.

I did not recognise myself because I have forgotten what I look like. I have not seen my reflection since I became trapped here.

She couldn't think of a single response. She couldn't imagine forgetting what you looked like. It made sense though. If all the mirrors of your world showed another world you couldn't use them as mirrors. Mattie remembered the day she'd seen him on the stairs. He had not been reflected in the other mirror. How awful.

Suddenly a knocking at her bedroom door broke her reverie and Jonathan opened the door.

"Mattie, a couple of us are going skating at the ice rink. Would you care to join us?"

"Um…"

Bastian was still in the mirror as Jonathan came into the room but Jonathan apparently couldn't see him.

"Come on. You've barely been out of the house since you came here. It's about time you saw the sights Dunmore has to offer."

"I've never skated before."

"Brilliant. One of my specialties is breaking in virgins. You might want to change into jeans though. Meet you downstairs when you're ready. We'll take the Jag."

Apparently taking it as a forgone conclusion that Mattie was joining them, Jonathan left the room, shutting the door behind him.

> Jonathan wants me to go skating.
>
> *I will still be here upon your return.*
>
> Bastian.
>
> *Yes Matilda.*
>
> Feel free to look through the sketch book. There are several of you in there.
>
> *Thank you.*

Chapter Six

With a groan Mattie staggered out of bed. She ached everywhere. She didn't consider herself unfit but after last night she was willing to rethink her verdict. Muscles were aching that she hadn't known she possessed. The skating rink had provided knee and elbow pads but with the amount of falls she'd taken her legs and arms were bruised all over. Looking into the mirror as she washed her face, she saw a graze on her cheekbone over a nasty blue bruise.

"You should see the other fella." She muttered and winced as the graze stung with the water. Her hands were grazed as well and she could just hear her agents reprimand.

"What were you thinking? Mattie dear, how could you put your hands at risk like that? Grazes are one thing but what if you lost a finger? One errant skate could mean the end of your livelihood. Must I do all your thinking for you?" Mattie mimicked.

Clarinda was a wonderful agent, understanding and lenient, but she had an annoying tendency to be overprotective of her investments, and Mattie knew her talent to draw was one of Clarinda's prized investments. She'd been told so many times.

Mattie wiggled her fingers at the imaginary Clarinda.

"See, ten."

Drying her face gingerly on the washcloth she tossed it in the basket as she walked past, and glanced at the clock on her side table. It was five-thirty in the morning. Crawling back under the blankets she propped herself up with the pillows. She wasn't tired. Her gaze fell upon the puzzle box on the side table, behind the clock, where she'd put it last night. Reaching for it she jumped a mile when the phone suddenly rang, causing her to knock the box onto the floor with a loud clatter. Snatching the phone she hit talk before it occurred to her that as a guest she probably shouldn't be answering the phone.

"Uh… Ashcombe residence." She said as she knelt on the floor to pick up the pieces of the puzzle.

"Who is this?"

"My name is Mattie, I'm staying here for a while. May I take a message?"

"It's Alex."

"Oh, hi Alex. Jonathan is still asleep."

"Big night?"

"Sort of. It's five-thirty."

"In the morning? Sorry about that. We thought it would be about eight."

Mattie heard him relay the time to someone.

"Hang on, your mother wants to talk to you."

She waited for the phone to be passed along.

"Hi Mattie. Sorry for the wakeup call, I got the time differences wrong."

"That's alright. I was awake already. How are you?"

"I'm fine, wonderful, great, terrific, well I'm sure you get the idea. Anyway we just rang to let you know the details of our flight. Have you got a pen?"

Mattie grabbed the nearest pen and copied down the details.

"DCF 1037, Monday the 29th of November at eleven am. Got it. Now is that eleven am, my time or your time?"

Crystal laughed. "London time. I'll let you go, Alex wants to take me shopping."

"Have fun."

"Will do. Bye."

"Bye."

Mattie hung up the phone and picked up the puzzle box from the floor. From the looks of things she might have broken it. The box had four little balls at each corner that acted as feet and one of them looked ready to fall off. Sitting back on the bed she inspected it closely. She had some glue in her art kit. No sooner did she have that thought than she saw that the foot screwed on. Twisting it anti-clockwise the ball came off into her hand and to her surprise the ball was attached to a little key. Tilting the box she looked at all four drawers. Each of the drawers had elaborate drawings of animals but none of them had a key hole.

She ran her hand over the entire box. There didn't appear to be a key hole anywhere. Mattie turned on the lamp and tilted it to shine directly on the box then held the key up to the light. There was an inscription on the end. Fumbling in her art kit she took out the magnifying glass and saw the inscription was in fact a ladybird. She flipped the box around and sure enough one of the drawings was a ladybird. Logically she concluded that the key was for that drawer but how did she unlock it? Hesitantly she tried the drawer but it was locked and didn't open. She looked at the key in her hand and at the drawer again. Slowly she twisted the drawer handle anti-clockwise.

It turned.

When it came off in her hand she inserted the key where the handle had been.

It fit.

Holding her breath Mattie turned the key to the right and was rewarded by the metallic sound of an opening lock. Using the ball of the key as the handle the drawer opened easily. The inside of the drawer was lined in red velvet but was otherwise empty. It didn't matter to her that it was empty. She'd figured out how to open the drawers. The puzzle was nothing more than a decoration. Closing the drawer she tipped the box upside down and tried to turn the next foot. It didn't budge. After a moment Mattie relocked the drawer and swapped the key for the handle, then replaced the key in its original place.

Trying again she turned the next foot and the key came out easily into her hand. This key had the inscription of a snake. She found the correct drawer and opened it. It was lined again in red velvet only this time the drawer also had a silver backed hand mirror. It was beautiful. The whole thing was etched with rose vines complete with thorns and leaves but instead of rose buds or flowers there were little fairy faces peeking out of the bushes. At the very back of the mirror in the middle of the rose vine was the Ashcombe family crest. Placing it on the bed Mattie opened the next drawer, a horse, and found a rectangular black leather box.

She gave a low whistle as she opened it. Nestled inside lay what looked to be a slender diamond and blue Sapphire bracelet set in either silver or white gold with a matching set of earrings. Closing the jewellery box she set about opening the fourth drawer and found a bound writing book covered in black cloth. The pages were unlined and stiff to turn. She opened to the first page. The cursive writing was difficult to read and the ink had faded in places to near illegible.

> *To my ....,*
>
> *This book is for your .... ideas.*
>
> *Ideas can .... a fire of the .... forever*
>
> *Mummy*

A book from a mother to her child.

Mattie flipped through it and started reading where the book automatically opened near the middle of the second half of the book. The writing on the following pages was easier to read.

> *When does a female change from delightful and innocent girl to plain and dull woman. Outwardly they change to delicate temptations of the senses, butterflies of gaiety and laughter but inwardly their minds dull, and there is no idea in their pretty little heads but for the entrapment of a husband and the manipulation of his good humour.*
>
> *Duty dictates that I wed by my birthday next, bound to a woman whose existence is*

*wholly for the next function, and the
clothing of the season.*

*Horror unbounded. Surly there be a woman
fair whose mind is full of other than such
simple nothings. A woman who knows her
mind yet is mindful of her husband's
position. A woman to whom conversation is
more than a fluttering of eyelashes and high
pitched giggles. God is yet to create such a
creature I fear. So onto the morrow and the
next paraded beauties, each as plain and dull
as the next.*

Mattie turned to the next page curious to see if
he found the woman he was looking for.

Yet another tedious day passes.

*BK eased the tedium a little but I am so
weary of this continued parade. Their faces
all blur into nothing. Red, blonde, brunette
they all appear the same. One quoted
Browning today, I grew hopeful of a
glimmer, when upon further inspection she
had merely known the words of the poetry
and nothing of the meaning, nor did she
show an enthusiasm to learn.*

*Perhaps it is best if I no longer endure this
endless torture and have Mother and Father
choose for me as they have threatened so oft.
Percy is of no help. He merely urges me to
make up my mind as quickly as I can so he
may wed his sweetheart.*

*How I envy his position. As second son he
enjoys the luxury of choosing for love.*

> *What is love? It is said that to find love one must look in, not out. I am to know it not. I must wed for suitability. Suitability for child bearing, an heir must be born, suitable breeding, suitable rearing, a woman who knows how a household is run. A woman who cares nothing for me, but is suitable for the title of Ashcombe.*

She read on.

> *The bell tolls and it sends shivers through my bones. Time has caught me. At this time tomorrow I am to announce my bride at my birthday ball. I am nothing but a prize to be fought for and won.*
>
> *I bear the scars to prove it.*
>
> *There are many who would be sport in the bedroom, they have already offered a taste of their charms. If I am to find them of such value, are there not other men who will find them the same?*
>
> *Genteel, well-mannered <u>strumpets</u>.*
>
> *They tease, offer, manipulate and twist so as to overshadow the competition. It would amuse if it were not I who were in the web.*
>
> *What horrors will the morrow bring? I feel as though led to the gallows.*

Mattie quickly turned the page.

> *The deed is done.*

That was it. The next page was blank, and the next and the next. There was no more writing in the book. What sort of ending was that? She flipped to the beginning of the book. Holding the page up to the light she read the inscription again, this time turning the book this way and that in the light until she could make out the inscription fully.

> *To my dear Bastian,*
>
> *This book is for your dreams and ideas.*
>
> *Ideas can light a fire of the imagination that burns forever.*
>
> *Mummy*

Mattie stared at the book in her hands in disbelief. She should have recognised the hand writing. What were the odds that she would find Bastian's diary? It wasn't really a diary in the traditional sense of the word, as he had only written in it occasionally. It was an account that ran in fits and starts, from Bastian's childhood up to that last page. The first pages were the adventures of childhood which led to the confusion of adolescence and the introduction of girls. He'd written that he was going to University then there was nothing for six years.

Obviously he hadn't taken the diary to Uni with him. When he started writing in it again he confessed to a passion for the performing arts that his family discouraged, so he became the Patron of the theatre company in Dunmore to see all the shows. There was a large succession of women referred to only by their initials and a great insight into his thoughts on various topics and people, but there was nothing more on his wedding and certainly nothing on who he might have offended to become trapped in the mirror.

Biting her lip she tried to push it to the back of her mind. One day, shortly, she really had to ask him. Once she screwed up the courage that was. For some reason it was so hard to put the question to paper. Picking up the mirror she turned it slowly in her hand with a frown. A portable mirror. Jumping out of bed she sat at the dresser and flipped back through their exercise book.

I have not seen the garden for many years. There are no mirrors there.

If Bastian could flit from mirror to mirror then conceivably he could go into the hand mirror and she could take him into the garden. Placing the puzzle box, jewellery box, diary and mirror in the top drawer of the dresser she raced into the bathroom and, after throwing a towel over the bathroom mirror, had a quick shower. She was still drying her hair when she came back to the dresser mirror but it didn't look like Bastian had been. There was no writing in the exercise book. Placing the items in the top drawer Mattie quickly twisted her hair into a knot and clamped it with a crab clip before tapping on the glass of the mirror. After three attempts and no response she took the hand mirror and sketch pad with her and went in search of Bastian.

Jonathan stumbled out of his room, wearing nothing but jeans he'd so obviously just pulled on, as Mattie went past.

"How long have you been up?" He asked, taking in her freshly scrubbed appearance.

"Since five-thirty."

"Are you mad?"

"No…" She laughed. "Our parents called. I've got their flight details."

"Oh good." Jonathan said without enthusiasm. "What are your plans?"

"Nothing much."

"Good, you can help me choose a wine."

"Choose a wine?"

"Marcus' birthday party tonight. He likes wine so I thought I'd give him a selection from our cellar."

"Marcus? You mean the Marcus from last night, the blond bloke?"

"Yes. You should come."

"I'd only know you. That wouldn't be much fun."

"You know Marcus. He thought you were pretty cute."

"Does he need glasses or something?"

"No." Jonathan laughed. "Come now you must admit that you are."

"What, in need of glasses?"

"No, cute."

"You make me sound like a puppy."

"Fine then, you're kind of hot."

Mattie blew a raspberry in disbelief. "If you think that, you need to have your eyes checked. I've done my self-portrait enough times to know that is not true. There is nothing extraordinary about me at all."

"That's just it. Nothing sticks out wrongly or is over proportionate. Everything about you fits perfectly with everything else. But more than that, nothing about you is forced or false. You have a natural beauty that is so refreshing, particularly amongst the woman I know."

"Oh." She couldn't think of anything else to say. No one had ever described her like that before. She had always thought herself plain and boring.

Jonathan simply laughed and opened the door to the dining room.

"Come on, I'm in the mood for pancakes. What are you having?"

Chapter Seven

Jonathan led Mattie to the bottom of a staircase with his hands coving her eyes. She held tightly to her art kit, she'd only just had time to safely encase the mirror inside. Jonathan hadn't even given her a chance to put it back in her room before he'd dragged her into an elevator and told her to close her eyes.

"Ta da." He announced.

Mattie blinked in the muted light and looked around her with a low whistle. In every direction she looked were racks filled with rows and rows of bottles of wine. There must have been thousands.

"This is some cellar."

"It's nothing fancy…" Jonathan shrugged with a mischievous glint. "… but it is adequate."

"Are you sure it's big enough?"

"I'd admit it's a tad cramped but one must make do."

Mattie laughed and shook her head at his suddenly toffish accent. He unplugged a pad from under the stairs.

"What's with that?"

"It's the data base. How else do you expect to find any wine down here? You'd be down here for months otherwise."

She could only agree as he typed a few words on the screen.

"This way."

As she trotted along behind him she couldn't get over the quantity of wine and the size of the cellar. She wouldn't say she was a wine connoisseur but she recognised some labels from back home and it wasn't the cheap stuff. A soft white light came from her left and she paused to investigate. The light came from a line of six fridges with glass fronts and all filled with wine. She could only laugh in astonishment. They even had them ready chilled. Turning around she found she'd lost Jonathan. A quick search revealed that he was a few shelves up and had, somewhere along the way, collected a basket with six compartments for wine bottles. She stood next to him as he grabbed a bottle of red and put it into his basket. Frowning slightly she ran her fingers over the nearest row of bottles. There wasn't a speck of dust to be found.

"How do you keep this place so clean?"

"Most of it is because of the design of the room, but like everything it does get dusted occasionally."

"You're kidding me, right?"

"No."

"Who could ever drink so much wine?"

Jonathan laughed. "The Ashcombe's have been collecting wine since Caleb Ashcombe."

"Caleb? He was the third Ashcombe to live at the Manor, wasn't he? Walter's son."

"Yes, very good. But you couldn't drink all of the wine down here anyway."

"Why not?"

"It's too old; it would have turned to vinegar by now."

"Really?"

"Yes."

"So why do you keep it."

"As an investment. Some of the older wines are worth hundreds of thousands of pounds."

"Ye gads, for vinegar?"

"No not for vinegar. For the label and unopened bottle."

Mattie could only stare at him. "Rich people are crazy."

"No, my dear. Poor people are crazy, rich people are eccentric."

"Semantics."

"Do you want to see an eccentricity that blew your mother's mind?"

"It would have to be history related." Mattie guessed. Her mum could get excited by looking at household accounts from the turn of last century.

"Of course."

Jonathan led her to the far end of the shelving unit. It was quite a hike and Mattie could understand why it would take months to find a bottle of wine. At the end was a large expanse of brick wall and when Jonathan led her down for what felt like miles they came to a huge safe door. She could well imagine that it would take four men to open it, it was so big. Punching in numbers on a panel to the right of the door Jonathan waited a moment and with a deep thud followed by lots of higher pitched noises the door slowly swung inwards. Staring at the thickness she revised her estimate of how many men it would take to open the door. Un-powered the door had to weigh tons. Undaunted Jonathan stepped into the vault. She followed him in and could see sensors everywhere.

"What are they for?" She asked pointing.

"Some are for security and some are for keeping the room at a constant environment, but that isn't what I wanted to show you. Come and see this."

The vault was smaller by far than the cellar, but it was still a large room. It too boasted rows and rows of wine bottles. Jonathan went to the end of the very last row and handed her a bottle of wine. The bottle was brown glass and looked nothing like the bottles that were used for wine now days. Carefully she turned it to read the label. It was faded cream and sepia tones and the script was hard to read but after a moment she made it out.

"Caleb Ashcombe. The year of our Lord 1553, October fifteenth. Wow."

"If you look here." Jonathan pointed. "You'll see that the wine is actually made in October 1553."

"That's old. Vinegar right?"

"Yes vinegar. Every male in the Ashcombe line has a bottle."

"What? Not just the first born?"

"No, all of them."

"Is it some kind of tradition like the mirrors?"

Jonathan shrugged. "I guess so."

Mattie made her way slowly down the row of bottles. Even though she ran her fingers lightly over every one she was looking for one in particular. Soon she found it.

Sebastian Ashcombe, 29 February 1836.

Frowning she stopped short and reread the label. It definitely read 29 not 28.

"Jonathan. I think this label is wrong."

"Really? Why?"

"If memory serves me correctly I think Sebastian was born on the twenty-eighth of February not the twenty-ninth."

"Is the year correct?"

"Yes."

Jonathan read the label and shrugged. "Twenty-eight, twenty-nine, what does a day matter?"

"What does it matter? It means it's wrong. Or if it's right then the history books are wrong."

"I thought you didn't like history. Why are you getting so upset?"

"You don't care that what you are telling people about your own family history is a lie?"

"Whoa, Mattie. Take it easy. It's just a day."

"How would you feel if in a hundred years people say you were born in April and not August?"

"In a hundred years I'll be dead, I wouldn't care." Jonathan laughed. "What is the big deal?"

"It doesn't matter. You wouldn't understand." She had to calm down. He was right, she was taking it all out of proportion but she couldn't help it.

"Try me." He said gently taking her by the shoulders and turning her to face him.

For a moment she hesitated trying to think of how she could best explain without Jonathan thinking she'd lost her marbles.

"I've been doing some research on your family history and there is a stack of information on almost every single one of your ancestors bar one. Sebastian Ashcombe. It's almost like someone has tried to erase him from your family line. I can find four pieces of information on him from the reference book in your library and one of those four pieces is his date of birth. If it's wrong then you've got next to nothing on the man. I mean there isn't even any mention that he was Patron of the Dunmore theatre from 1859 to 1869."

"How do you know that if there is no mention of it?"

"There is no mention of it in your family history books but there is a mention of it at the Dunmore Theatre." Mattie explained, thankful she had taken the time to check it out after Bastian mentioned it.

"Mattie?"

"Yes?"

"I thought you hated history."

"I do."

"Then why are you researching my family tree? Are you looking for skeletons?"

"No. Not skeletons, not really."

Suddenly Jonathan burst out laughing so hard he doubled over clutching his stomach.

"I don't believe it." He gasped. "Steady, no-nonsense Mattie Holmes is investigating the Ashcombe curse."

"What's so funny about that?" She demanded jamming her hands on her hips.

"You won't be able to do it."

"Why not? I'm good at puzzles. I figured out that puzzle box of yours."

His head shot up.

"Was there anything in it?"

"Yes. A mirror, some jewellery and a… an old style… uh notebook." For some reason she tried to play down Bastian's diary.

"Are you serious?"

"Yes. Still think I won't be able to solve the curse?"

"I don't know. What have you found out so far?"

Mattie blinked. She hadn't been expecting the question.

"That much?"

"The rhyme you quoted as being the curse is wrong."

"And what is the correct rhyme pray tell."

"Ashcombe man thy vanity keeps thee, till love shines beauty in purity, till shattered heart within pierce free, and with single breath, mirror pass'ed be."

"That is a little more poetic to say the least."

"That is exactly what I thought. Oh, on a side note I think Jemima Middleton is a made up ghost."

"Why do you say that?"

"Well she was supposed to have been jilted at the alter by her betrothed in 1870 and as far as I can tell there was only one Ashcombe man of marriageable age in 1870, and that was Percival, but he married his childhood sweetheart Dallas Eldredge in July of 1869. His brother Sebastian was betrothed to Penelope Cranston earlier that same year and it could be said that she was jilted because he disappeared on their wedding day. Jemima isn't mentioned at all in the Ashcombe family tree and as far as I can find, all the male Ashcombes were married at the time except for Rafael, a Great-uncle who was seventy-two, and the sons of Bastian's sisters, the oldest being eleven or so. So unless her betrothed was not an Ashcombe, and she happened into the garden to drown herself, then she is a made up ghost."

Jonathan gave her a strange look. "I thought you said you were no good at history."

"I'm not. I only reread it today."

The conversation was on the same page as Bastian's comment about the gardens.

"Anything else?"

"Um, there is no mention of the curse before 1869."

"Nothing written anyway."

"I don't think it existed before then. Think about it. Your family is famous in these parts and you have so much history around here. Don't you think someone would have written the curse down before the Nineteenth century if it existed?"

"1869? Didn't you say Percival's brother, Samuel ..."

"Sebastian."

"... Sebastian disappeared about that time?"

"Yes." Mattie held her breath and waited. Was it possible Jonathan would guess what she knew? It would be great if he did. Then it would be his own idea that Bastian was the cursed Ashcombe. Perhaps she would be able to lay it all out and have someone else's thoughts to help solve the mystery.

"Perhaps the curse was created to cover his disappearance."

"Not cover it. It was because of it. You say the Manor is haunted by ghosts, I say it's haunted but not by a ghost and the rhyme is the clue on how to break the curse."

"To quote what you said the other day, you are making as much sense as waterproof teabags."

"Bastian disappeared on his wedding day, so he is the obvious candidate and since the rhyme says 'vanity' I reckon it's got something to do with all the mirrors around here and what a perfect place to curse a man…"

Jonathan's laughter interrupted her train of thought and she trailed off.

"You've been speaking to Stacey haven't you?"

"Stacey?"

"Yes Stacey. She says she can see a man in the mirror. Don't tell me you've swallowed her cock-and-bull story about that have you?"

Mattie almost dropped the art kit in surprise.

"Stacey can see a man in the mirror?"

"Yes, out of the corner of her eye and all that. Don't look at me like that. She has obviously told you otherwise you wouldn't have come to such a conclusion about the curse. A man in the mirror, please, that is just so naff."

"Stacey never told me she could see a man in the mirror."

"So you came up with that all by yourself?" He laughed.

"Yes, and if all you can do is laugh at me I'm going up stairs."

"Oh come on Mattie don't be like that. It is a strange coincidence."

"No it is not." Mattie stormed from the vault

"Mattie. I apologise for teasing you. I had no idea you felt so passionate about this."

She glared at him then sighed. To be honest she felt more betrayed by Bastian's omission than Jonathan's teasing.

"It's okay. I'm sorry I got so mad."

"Apology accepted. Talk to me about it, only start from the beginning because I think you've started your explanation partway through. Now as I understand it you think the curse is real and there is a man - Sebastian Ashcombe, my ancestor - who is trapped in the mirror, and the rhyme explains how he can break the curse."

"Yes."

"What else?"

"That's about it."

"Okay." He said slowly. "So why do you think the rhyme will break the curse?"

"Ashcombe man thy vanity keeps thee, *till* love shines beauty, purity, *till* shattered heart within pierce free. Until these things happen then Bastian is trapped.”

“Well having all these mirrors around can’t be a great help.”

“How do you mean?”

“ ‘… thy vanity keeps thee…’ With all these mirrors about his vanity would be constantly pandered to.”

“But he can’t see his reflection.”

“Why would you think that?”

Mentally Mattie kicked herself for her slip. “It makes sense for him not to be able to. I mean if Stacey can see him in the mirror, then mirrors would conceivably be more like windows for him and not mirrors.”

“If you say so.” Jonathan said sounding not at all convinced.

“I say so.”

“Answer something for me?”

“What?”

“How can a single breath pass a mirror?”

Mattie stood straighter and stared at him. “So you believe me?”

“Let me just say I’m reserving judgement until I hear all you have to say. However you can’t be an Ashcombe and not entertain a certain curiosity about the curse.”

“ ‘…With single breath mirror pass’ed be.’” Mattie rested her chin on her fingers as she thought about it. “I have no idea. The only thing that I can think of is the fog you get when you breathe on a mirror, but it doesn't pass through."

"None of it makes any sense. I've never been able to figure it out and I've known about the curse since I was in shorts."

"Last summer?"

"No. It's a saying. It means, since I was younger. Since I was in short coats is the full saying, but it's rather old-fashioned these days. Come on. We are supposed to be collecting wine bottles." He said pressing a button which swung the vault door closed, and passing her the handheld screen. "It will go faster if we both gather. You take this and I'll get another."

He gave her a quick lesson on how to use it and then left to get his own. Mattie stared after him amazed at how quickly he seemed to dismiss the curse. Shaking her head she went to her left looking for the shelving unit with a 'G' aisle as the screen directed her. Rounding the end of the nearest shelves she pressed too close and knocked a bottle off its perch. Grabbing quickly she manage to just catch it while still holding the computer and the art kit. Breathing a deep sigh of relief she carefully replaced the bottle then bent to retrieve the brushes that had spilled from her kit, hoping nothing breakable had fallen out. Still everything in her kit, except perhaps Bastion's mirror, was relatively cheap compared to a bottle of 1912 white.

To her annoyance several brushes had rolled under the shelving. All she needed now was to knock the whole shelf. Lying flat on the ground she carefully reached under the unit. To her surprise she saw a mirror in the shape of the Ashcombe crest embedded into the stone under the shelves. Who in their right mind would put a mirror *under* a shelf?

Most of the brushes were in reach, but one she could only reach with her fingertips. Wriggling her hand on the stone she stretched further and managed to gain a tentative hold on the bristles with the very ends of her fore and middle fingers. Curling her fingers to pull the brush closer the heel of her palm pressed directly over the mirror and to her great astonishment the mirror depressed.

From behind her came the quiet rasping of stone on stone. Unable to suppress a shudder at the sound, she quickly grabbed the brush and turned as she sat up. At the very corner of the cellar, where the join of two walls met, a crack had appeared. Without taking her eyes off it, she stepped closer. As she touched the wall she jumped when Jonathan called her name.

"Mattie? You haven't gone very far." He laughed as he came around the shelves.

"I uh…um the…w…" She stammered.

"Care to repeat that?"

"The w…"

"Yes?"

"The wine, I… uh almost smashed a bottle of wine and I… didn't want to risk touching any more of them." Mattie suddenly decided not to tell Jonathan about the wall. He probably knew about it anyway and as Stacey said, there were no secret entrances only servant ones.

"From the graceful way you move I would not believe you were a klutz, but after seeing you skate last night, well anything's possible."

"Do you take anything seriously?" Mattie asked as Jonathan placed his hand on the small of her back to guide her forward.

"Try not to, no." He laughed and dropped his hand as Mattie moved away. His touch was a little too intimate for her liking. He was starting to touch more and more frequently. Nothing sordid, but it made her feel uncomfortable all the same.

Chapter Eight

Jonathan had talked her into going to the party tonight but she still had a few hours to kill and knew exactly what she wanted to do in that time. Already in jeans, she changed from her white shirt into a darker one and switched from sandals to sneakers.

Taking the torch from the side table, she paused, realising how suspicious it would look walking around with it. Retrieving the art kit she rearranged it to fit the torch then left for the cellar.

Making it un-confronted she carefully pulled the wall open. A low doorway of sorts appeared. Tightening the straps on her art kit Mattie slung it over her shoulder and flicked on the torch following its beam of light into the darkness. The wall was about as thick as the door on the vault and she was glad she hadn't needed to pry it open by herself. Suddenly she heard a click and the wall rasped closed. Heart pounding she raced back, only to find herself shut in. Swinging the light around, she saw the glint of a mirror on the floor. It was the same as the Ashcombe crest under the shelves. Kneeling, she pressed it down in the centre and the wall reopened. Cautiously she stood and pressed down again with the toe of her sneaker. As she expected, the wall closed. She tried it several more times before she was convinced she wouldn't lock herself in.

Unlike the cellar, the small room she stood in lay under a thick layer of dust. In the thin beam of the torchlight she saw blank stone walls with one archway across the room. Slowly she stepped forward. Nothing in the room looked sinister but she'd seen 'Indiana Jones' one time too many and she didn't have a script to guide her.

It was lucky that she did take it carefully because suddenly, without any warning, the archway plunged down into stairs. Before Mattie took a single step, she shone the torch on all the cobwebs that stretched across the opening, and suppressed a shudder. While she wasn't particularly arachnophobic, she didn't know if England had poisonous spiders. The first two that flashed through her mind were the white tail and the red-back from home, both of which were very poisonous. Glancing behind her she saw nothing useful, so she resorted to using her hand to sweep part of the sticky mass away so that she could step down. Like the stairs at the servants' entrance the stone treads had worn indentations at the centre, however the walls were uncovered stone and every step sent up a puff of thick pale dust.

The stairs came to an end at a small rectangular room. There were cobwebs everywhere but not as thick as they'd been on the stairs. Her torch light showed her three doorways with wooden doors. Trying the door to her left she found it locked. Assuming the same of the door to her right she tried it anyway and to her surprise it opened slightly then stuck fast. Shining the torch through the gap she saw a flat wooden bench and a sliding wooden window at head height. A sagging mesh curtain hung down, torn, through the window. Her first thought was a toilet but there was no hole in the seat.

Stepping away she turned the beam of light to the two arched doors. On each door about chin height

a nail protruded where something once had hung.
Whatever it had been was long gone. Closing the gap
to the doors her foot kicked something on the floor.
Pointing the beam down, she swept it past a dark
object. Bending, she carefully picked it up and turned
it over. The wood was black with age and the copper
had long turned green and was half gone. There was
two pieces of frayed twine at the top and it was this
that had clearly fallen from the door. In the torch light
she could still see the remains of what had once been
a crucifix.

Jesus' legs were missing and so was the top of
his head. She could only just see his face. He looked
rather worse for wear. So the 'toilet' could
conceivably be a confessional, but she couldn't say
for sure. It felt wrong to put the crucifix back on the
floor so she knotted the twine and placed it back on
the nail As she let go Jesus fell from his cross leaving
only the three rusted nails behind, one where each
hand had been and one where his feet had been
attached.

"Jesus has left his cross." She muttered to
herself in a manner reminiscent of a departing Elvis
as her torch failed to find the copper figure even
though she'd heard it clunk and clatter on the stone.

Twisting the handle of the left door she
pushed. The door groaned loudly in protest but ever
so slowly gave way. Her first step placed her on
faded, and from the smell of it, mouldy red carpet. A
quick glance showed that she was most definitely in a
small chapel. To her right was an alcove with several
bookshelves that even had some books. The titles that
she could read proclaimed them Hymn and Prayer

books. To her left was another alcove but this housed what looked like an elaborate bird bath. Behind that was a tall flat cupboard. The left door of which was hanging loose and she could see, of all things, what looked like one of those hooked staff things that was used to drag dreadful people off stage in a comedy reel.

Her torch picked out several rows of wooden benches all dust covered and sagging. As she walked closer to the alter she saw a very large silver Ashcombe crest. It appeared to be at least seven feet high and some four or five feet wide. At first she thought it was mounted on the wall but she realised that the altar was behind it. Shining the torch above it she looked for the ropes or whatever that held it in place. Who in their right mind would put a crest that big in front of the altar? No one in the audience would be able to see the Pastor or whoever at the front. Walking slowly around it she was surprised not to see any struts or supports. Nor could she see any ropes or chains attached. How did it stay upright? Suddenly she had to jerk the torch away as she blinded herself.

"Bloody hell." She whispered carefully aiming the torch at the ground. It was one whopping great big mirror. Looking at her reflection she had to laugh. She looked like she had lost a round with a fairy floss machine. She was absolutely covered in spider web. Her laughter was cut short as she saw that some of what she'd taken as spider web on herself was actually writing etched into the glass. She had to round the other side of the altar and press herself against the wall and even then she could only just make out the words. What she read made her heart stop for a moment then with a mad scramble she unhooked her art kit and delved for a pencil and paper. Making absolutely certain she was copying it correctly she wrote down the words.

Ashcombe man thy vanity keep thee

Till Love shines Beauty in purity

Till shattered heart within pierce free

And with single breath, mirror pass'ed be

Ashcombe man in reflection thou wilt stay

Hidden in sight thy debt to pay

Until Four and Forty natal day

Thy existence ends and thy time fades away

There was no doubt in her mind that what she had was the entire curse. Now all she had to do was figure it out. Carefully keeping the beam of light at the edges of the mirror she re-read the inscription then sucked her bottom lip into her mouth. It felt wrong to do it but no one was watching. With a deep breath she clambered onto the dusty altar. The top of the mirror came to her chest but it was just out of reach. She quickly clambered down again and retrieved a chair. Trying her best not to knock it, she leaned as close as she dared and cautiously inspected the glass.

As far as she could tell there was no more writing, not a single inscription other than the two verses. Moving the chair, she turned her attention to the back. It was completely smooth except for the crest that rose a little like a negative imprint. At first it appeared to be simply the Ashcombe Crest, nothing unusual with it at all, but as she glanced down her passing gaze noted something unusual. Pausing a moment to regain her balance Mattie slowly looked it over again. Instead of a smooth edge like the rest of the crest's imprint the outside edge was ridged. Tilting her head she almost fell off the chair when she realised it was writing. Squinting she angled her head to make the words clearer.

"Walter Fredrick Ashcombe, William Michael Ashcombe, Leonard Christian Ashcombe, Sebastian Richard Ashcombe…" Mattie frowned trying to make out the final three words. They were faded and faint as if the oldest. "…Jonathan Gordon Ashcombe. Jonathan? I didn't know there was an earlier Jonathan. Walter Fredrick Ashcombe, William Michael Ashcombe, Leonard Christian Ashcombe, Sebastian Richard Ashcombe, Jonathan…" The same five names were repeated again and again to make up the entire edge of the crest.

Suddenly Mattie froze. These, except for the unknown Jonathan, were the names of all the Ashcombes who had disappeared. Did that mean that they had all been affected by the curse? But that would mean that the curse was around longer than she'd realised. It would certainly suggest that it had been around a lot longer than it had been recorded. Stepping quickly off the chair she abruptly sat. Sebastian said that he was cursed because he'd angered the gypsy nurse of his betrothed. How was that possible? The curse was obviously older than that. Instead of answering her questions this trip to the mirror only created more. About to rise, her torch flickered off the very lowest left corner edge. Leaning closer she read the strange encryption.

Зеркало

Chapter Nine

"You seem a little distracted." Jonathan said as he dumped his keys in the black glazed bowl in the foyer.

"Huh?"

Mattie had gone with Jonathan to Marcus' birthday but her mind had been on the curse all night. She couldn't stop thinking about the rhyme.

"Maybe little is an understatement. Don't tell me Marcus made such a big impression as that on you."

"Marcus? Oh no, Marcus was nice, the perfect gentleman."

Jonathan snorted disbelievingly. "I have never heard Marcus and gentleman in the same sentence before."

"Well it's true."

"Coffee?"

"Huh? Oh, no thanks. I think I'll head to bed."

"It's not midnight yet Cinderella." Jonathan pointed to the clock to prove his point.

"It's late enough. This Cinderella suffers from trying to adjust to the time difference."

"After all this time?"

"Yep."

Jonathan gave her a sad puppy dog look and took her hands in his pulling her closer. "I can't tempt you to change your mind?"

"Nope." Mattie pulled her hands away under the guise of straightening the waist of her skirt.

"Ah, well. Goodnight then." Swiftly Jonathan moved forward and, before she realised his intention, had kissed her. She jerked back.

"Don't do that Jonathan."

"Do what?"

"I'm not one of your girls, okay? Just ease up on the touching."

Jonathan shrugged. "It's just how I am."

"Yeah I know, just ease up will you. After all I am your sister."

"Step-sister."

"Still makes me related."

"Not by blood."

"Whatever. You know what I'm asking.

Crossing his arms Jonathan looked at her strangely "Have you ever had a boyfriend Mattie?"

"What sort of question is that?"

"Just curious."

"Yes I've had a boyfriend. Goodnight."

Mattie headed up the stairs.

"Have you ever had a man?"

Mattie tripped the step then looked down at him. He was standing there with his arms crossed.

"Goodnight Jonathan."

"Goodnight Mattie."

She heard his voice softly behind her but refused to turn around as she stalked the rest of the way.

Bastian watched Matilda ascend the stairs and his eyes narrowed as he saw Jonathan watching her as well. The look he gave her retreating form was not one a brother would give a sister. To see the casual way Jonathan had taken hold of her hands burned inside. The only saving grace was that Matilda had pulled away. She had said that they were step-siblings and he had believed her. Why had she lied to him?

He watched Jonathan muse as he stared at the empty staircase. He knew that look. Jonathan was pleased with himself and he only wore that look when it had a sexual nature. Abruptly he faded from the mirror wishing he could rid himself of the painful burn he felt. Jonathan had his choice of women from all over Dunmore and he had to woo the only one who could see Bastian. He didn't ask why, he knew why. Matilda was untried territory, an unconquered challenge. He would have done the same thing when he had been part of the solid world. So this was how the other men felt as they saw their fillies fall under his charms in the courting game. Matilda didn't seem to be encouraging Jonathan but she didn't seem to be rebuffing him either.

Appearing in her dresser mirror he waited for her to enter her room. She came directly to the dresser and began writing.

> Why didn't you tell me
> Stacey could see you?

About to write his own question about Jonathan, her question threw him. He didn't know a Stacey.

> *Who is Stacey?*
>
> Stacey - the maid.
>
> *Which maid?*

Dark hair, hazel eyes, larger then I am, cleans the mirrors.

His frown cleared as it dawned on him who she meant.

I thought her name to be Masiy. She does not see me as you see me. Occasionally she will take a second glance however she never reacts in any way when I stand directly before her.

Mattie read his words then slowly nodded.

Did you not tell me that Jonathan and you are step-siblings?

Yes.

Your caresses appear to be peculiarly intimate for such a relationship.

Bastian lifted his eyes and studied her reaction. Her eyebrows rose suddenly then a slow smile crossed her face.

Interesting.

If I didn't know better I would say you're jealous.

Bastian gritted his teeth and swallowed hard. He was *not* jealous.

Jonathan is a tactile person, he touches everyone. Yes I would say particularly women, but then I've never seen him in the company of a man so I can't compare.

You have no objections to such actions?

Some of them.

Then why do you allow it?

I don't allow it particularly. Jonathan is just being Jonathan. He doesn't mean anything by it.

"I am not assured of that." Bastian said to himself, but he didn't write anything. She was right. He did sound jealous. That wasn't like him. He'd never been jealous of anything in his life, except perhaps the freedom from the curse that others enjoyed, freedom from the curse.

Bastian?

Yes Matilda.

I have a confession to make.

He waited without looking up, anticipating her next words.

Do you consider me a stranger?

No.

He wrote with a frown wondering what she could mean.

Good. Do you remember the other day when I got mad at you for looking at my sketch book without asking?

Yes.

As I said, it was understandable. I intruded into a private world of yours.

That's just it. I got mad at you, and then did exactly the same thing in return. I will understand if you are mad at me.

If you are attributing any drawings you may have found to me, I can assure you to be very much mistaken. I do not draw.

But you do write.

Before he could ask what she meant, she opened a drawer of the dresser. His hand went to the mirror in total surprise as she placed his treasure box on the top. The next moment he actually did stop breathing as she also set the mirror, the jewellery box and his journal next to it. Staring at the objects between them he tried to sort his swirling thoughts. He hadn't known anyone who could open the treasure box.

How did you open it?

I dropped it and the foot came off.

His head shot up in horror.

It's okay, it's not broken

Passing his hand through the ghostly reflections on the dresser he hovered over the journal and suddenly knew what she meant.

You've read my journal

Yes.

I'm so sorry Bastian. I had no idea it was yours. The handwriting is different, more fluid.

I am out of practice. Did I not say there was more to me than what you read in the family history book?

Yes you did.

Does this mean you aren't mad at me?

I am staggered to see that you have found this. I am not angry that you read the journal, truthfully I cannot remember exactly what I wrote as it was such a long time ago. I may be embarrassed later when I've reread it, but I am not angry. At this moment I am relieved more than I can say by the fact that I am not forgotten. You have the proof that I existed.

Concentrating hard he made a solid copy of the mirror and held it in his hand. He ran his palm over the back of it, feeling the indentation of the vines, faces and crest. He could remember describing the design to Percy who drew it so it could be created.

"Are you certain this is what you mean?"

"Absolutely."

"It is an odd choice, therefore I say it suits you perfectly. You do realise you are creating this for your bride and not yourself?"

"As I do not yet have a bride, it is I who decide the design.

"I can not understand why you are suddenly so particular."

"Would you so speedily choose a bride if it had to be one other than Dallas?"

"Hark, do you suggest that you have fallen for a woman of your own desire?"

"I suggest no such thing. I do suggest, however that you continue with your drawing or it will be your thirty-third birthday before you wed."

Slowly he turned it over and stared into the blackness where his reflection ought to have been. Closing his eyes he abruptly released the mirror. If only he had felt a glimmer of respect for Miss Cranston.

When he opened his eyes again he saw Mattie writing. His head was already aching and he realised that he'd released the book when he'd taken hold of the mirror. With his head pounding he solidified the book and the pen.

> Are you alright? Have I upset you?
>
> *Memories.*
>
> I'm sorry.
>
> *There is no need to be.*
>
> Is '3epkano' familiar to you?
>
> *It is a Russian word which means <u>Mirror</u>.*
>
> How do you pronounce it?

He had to think a moment for the best way to put it into writing.

> *Zerkano. It is also the name of a business in London which makes the mirrors for the Ashcombes. At least they did so while I was a part of your world.*

Matilda nodded.

> I found a mirror today and it has a second verse to the curse.

She opened a small notebook and began copying the verse he knew then followed with a second.

> *Intriguing, I do not know this second verse.*

Do you know what 'natal' means?

Birth. It can relate to place of birth or day of birth. I would suggest this refers to the latter.

Bastian, is your birthday the 28 or 29 of February?

Frowning Bastian hesitated.

I can not remember.

You can't remember?

No. I have no cause to celebrate it.

Matilda frowned then began writing numbers down the page. The first column looked like years from his year of birth and jumping every four years to twenty-twelve. Next to that she wrote 0, 4, 8 and so on all the way down and next to that 4, 8, 12, 16, again all the way down. She drew a circle around the number 1880 and a second circle around 2012.

Your birthday has to be 29 or you wouldn't be here.

How do you conclude this?

Read the last two lines of the 2nd verse.

"Until four and forty natal day, thy existence ends and thy time… fades… away." He stared down at the words again. "Fades away."

His headache thumped as the words sank in. Matilda was correct. His presence was the proof of his birth date. On his forty-fourth birthday he would simply cease to exist. As far as he knew he hadn't aged but the years passed unrelentingly by.

We have less than a year to work out
how to get you out of there.

Where is this mirror? The one containing the verses?

In an old chapel that you get to by the
wine cellar.

Bastian frowned.

I know naught of a wine cellar.

I think it used to be servants quarters.

He knew of a chapel off the servants quarters, in fact he had reason to know it well, it's seclusion was ideal for… several things.

There is no mirror in the chapel.

There is. It's huge, and the back of it
has the Ashcombe crest. The edge of
the crest is made up of five names,
yours included.

Which reminds me, which Ashcombe was
the first Jonathan?

Blinking at her change of topic Bastian thought for a moment.

This Jonathan is the first.

That's impossible. I'll show you. Meet
you at the mirror.

"Matilda." He said uselessly as she stood.

Taking something from the drawer next to her bed she left the room. He didn't know which mirror she meant. Absently he rubbed at the pain in his temple. He knew every room the mirrors showed and not one of them showed the chapel. Abruptly he raised his head. Surely she didn't mean *that* mirror. Slowly he stood, then quickly made his way towards it. It was a sizeable mirror being larger than a man and it did display the crest at its back. It was a hated thing and he had deliberately tried to forget its existence. Steeling himself he forced his way around to the front.

"Please God." He prayed. "Do not allow her to mean this mirror."

Gritting his teeth he lowered his head and closed his eyes. He would wait here for a count of fifty but he doubted he could endure more than that. Taking a breath he solidified before the mirror and winced as the indiscernible hissing began. It was as if a thousand dead things whispered his secret sins, intent on making him relive every one of them. He could never understand what they said but he despised the sound. The glass was blacker than any night he had ever seen and it had always been that way. Nothing ever showed from this mirror and he wasn't sure he wanted to see anything it might reveal.

At the thirty-seventh count something unusual occurred. A sharp agonizing stab of pain hit behind his eyes but the hissing abruptly faded into the normal distorted distant sound of everything else in this prison. Opening his eyes he slowly lifted his head.

Matilda was standing before him.

Darkness surrounded her and he could see nothing of the chapel but she was clearly there. She smiled and curtsied. Automatically he returned with a bow but he was too stunned for anything else. Of everything he'd experienced in this prison this was one of the most unnerving, even more amazing than the day he'd solidified his first item. What did this mean? How did she appear in this God-forsaken mirror? Suddenly a wave of nausea crashed over him and the pain in his head intensified. There was only one way to ease the pain and he allowed himself to fade from the mirror.

Chapter Ten

It takes considerable effort to solidify objects and at times I find it exhausting. That was one such time.

She read the words as they appeared on the page with a slight smile. Sometimes she could imagine the sound of his voice. His accent would have to be like the ones in an Oscar Wilde play or a Jane Austen movie, very correct and every word carefully pronounced.

It is not easy to explain.

In a way. It is more as if I memorise a sense of the object. I do not need to know how it feels to touch nor the weight nor anything of its physical nature.

As I said it is not easy to explain. I do not imagine it in the creative definition of the word nor do I remember the object as a recollected memory. It is as if I hold the awareness of the object in my mind and force it to the point where it erupts into reality.

No, and though the latter is correct I too refer to the event as the former.

What?

There is no effort required in viewing the solid Manor. It merely appears and fades as I wish it. While I have view of your world there is a feeling over my body as if near pins and needles. When the vision fades so too does the feeling, therefore I refer to the occurrence as if it is I who fade, not the view in the mirror.

Weird.

It did take time to accustom myself to the sensation.

Mattie laughed then turned at the knock on her door.

"Yes?"

Jonathan opened the door and poked his head into the room.

"Apologies for interrupting the beauty routine but if we are to arrive on time we need to leave."

"Yep okay. Be down in a tick."

I have to go now.

Are you going out?

Yes. Jonathan and I are picking our respective parents up from the airport.

Airport?

Do you remember I told you about airplanes?

Yes. The machines that carry people as they fly.

The airport is the place where airplanes arrive and depart. Like a train station.

I see. Enjoy yourself. I will be here upon your return.

You'd better be.

She ended by drawing a quick smiley face, grabbed her jacket and the paper with the flight details, and bounded down the stairs. Jonathan was standing in the middle of the entertainment room riveted by the TV.

"Come on I thought you said we would be late."

"Shh Mattie, listen."

"…so far no survivors have been found. The debris from the wreckage spreads over five hundred meters and rescue workers have a hard task ahead of them. Emergency workers from all over England are being called upon to assist in the recovery efforts for this tragedy. More than one hundred and twenty passengers and crew members are yet to be accounted for. We don't know yet what caused the crash of flight DCF 1037 just moments ago, details are sketchy and we will bring you more news on this tragedy as they become available…"

Mattie didn't hear the rest of the reporters words as she stared at the pictures of the burning wreck in absolute horror.

"No." She whispered, unable to form a coherent thought.

"Good God Mattie, it's not…"

Silently, Mattie held out the note with the flight details as she stared in stunned disbelief at the TV.

Jonathan reached behind her and punched a number into the phone. He put it to his ear for a moment then redialled.

"All I'm getting is his voicemail. What's your Mother's number?"

Mattie tried to think of the number but all she could see was the twisted pieces of metal and scattered luggage littering the English countryside.

"Mattie, the number."

She took the phone with trembling hands and jerkily hit the buttons.

"G'day…"

"Mum?"

"…this is Crystal Day you've reached my voicemail. Please leave…"

Mattie hung up and redialled.

"Voicemail." She said as Jonathan looked at her expectantly. "They would have had to turn the phones off for the flight."

Jonathan took the phone and swore, running his hand through his hair. Punching more numbers he made another call.

"Sandy? It's Jonathan… Yes I know I just saw it on TV, that's why I'm calling… Can you tell me any more than what is being broadcast?... Any small detail?... Sandy, my father was on that flight… Yes… No, no. Have you heard anything about survivors? ... Okay… Yeah I'm fine, just let me know the instant you hear anything… You know my number… Bye. That was Sandy, she works at Channel Two. She doesn't know anything more than what they're broadcasting."

"Is there a one, eight hundred number or something for relatives to call?" Mattie asked. "They always scrolled a number at home for emergencies like this."

Jonathan stood next to her and watched the TV for a moment.

"Doesn't appear to be. Look, I'm going to make a few more calls and see if I can find out anything."

Mattie watched him leave the room punching more numbers into the phone. There was nothing she could do. She didn't know anyone, she couldn't call anyone who would know anything. Tears rolled down her cheeks as she stared numbly at the images on the screen. How could anyone survive that? There was almost nothing recognizable as a plane. She felt almost physically sick as more footage was shown and the carnage was explicitly revealed. Turning away she made her way slowly to her room and sat heavily at the dresser. It seemed a lifetime ago that she had drawn the carefree smiley on the page. Looking at the clock showed it had been less than fifteen minutes.

Gently she rested her hand on the glass of the mirror, closing her eyes with a sigh. She'd come upstairs to confide and look for comfort from Bastian, forgetting that he wasn't a physical part of her world. He'd become so much a part of her life that for a moment she expected him to be there able to provide the shoulder she needed right now.

"Bastian." She whispered.

Chapter Eleven

Startled, Bastian spun to look behind him.
"Hello? Is anyone there?"

No one was there, yet he could have sworn he had heard his name. It had been soft, a whisper, but so clear. He was positive it was a woman's voice. He waited, his eyes searching the dimly lit darkness for any movement, but there was nothing. The voice didn't repeat.

Choosing the nearest mirror he concentrated and saw Jonathan speaking into the handpiece of the telephone. Odd, why was he speaking to the telephone and not leaving the house? Fading from the mirror he moved onto the next and saw a huddle of maids in the kitchen, some of them were crying. With a frown he faded from that mirror and appeared in the mirror of Matilda's dresser. She wasn't there. Closing his eyes he solidified the dresser and their writing book with its pen. She'd written more. He read the page with a rising sense of hopelessness. He could read her grief in the words and wished he could do something for her. From his observances over the years, he knew that most women would collapse with grief and that they needed to allow this to happen first before they could move on to deal with what needed to be done. Men on the other hand dealt with things first and then grieved later.

He couldn't even hold her as she cried. Releasing the dresser he began searching the rooms of the 'solid' Manor for her. It was only after he had searched the rest of the Manor that he determinedly looked into *that* mirror. She was sitting before it with her arms wrapped around her middle, rocking. Her presence muted the hisses and even knowing she wouldn't hear him didn't stop him uttering her name.

"Matilda."

She lifted her head as if she did hear him and he saw her lips form his name. Unfolding to her feet she closed the gap to the mirror. He placed his hand against the glass wishing he could reach out and hold her. Mimicking his movements she placed her hand against where his rested. He'd known his share of grief as he'd seen his family members, one by one, succumb to the passing of time; and he knew what it was to have no comfort. He watched helplessly at the trail of the tears down her face as she rested her forehead near her hand. She was so near and yet he couldn't even wipe away her tears. He couldn't bear seeing her like this. With her peculiar turn of phrase and unique way of seeing things, she had become a bright beam of light in this dark world of his. He had never felt like this about anyone before. He felt almost consumed with the need to comfort her, to be her strength until she could stand on her own once again. Slowly he removed his hand from the glass; there was nothing he could do.

Suddenly they both jumped away from the mirror as the glass between them rippled. He had never seen anything like it. Cautiously he touched the glass. It was the same as always.

Matilda must have moved the mirror from her side though the ripple had never occurred when the mirrors had been moved about before. Bastian lifted a

shoulder to indicate that he had absolutely no idea
what had just happened. Matilda shook her head then
stepping closer to the mirror returned her hand to the
glass. To his absolute amazement, instead of halting,
her hand passed through the mirror before she
snatched it back with a look of shock. Reacting fast
he put his hands to the mirror but no matter where he
came into contact with it the glass it didn't yield.
Biting her lip Matilda slowly put her hand to the
mirror again. This time instead of snatching it back
she followed it… into his world. His hand had been
against the mirror during the entirety of her entrance,
yet the mirror had remained firm beneath his touch.
For a moment they simply stared at each other. He
couldn't think of a single word to say. Matilda moved
first. Turning around she reached out to the mirror
and watched her hand pass through the glass before
returning her gaze to him.

"Hello Bastian." She said with a faint smile.

He could hear the slight tremble in her voice
and her accent was not one he recognised. Suddenly
his breath left him so completely it was as if she had
slammed into his solar plexus. He could hear her.
Slowly he took a step closer and tentatively placed his
fingers on her cheek afraid she was a figment of his
imagination and would disappear. When she
remained real under his hand he gently used his
thumb to wipe away her tears marvelling at the
sensations: the wetness of her tears and the warmth of
her skin.

"Bastian." She whispered.

Closing the gap between them she wrapped
her arms around his shoulders and laid her cheek

against his chest holding him tightly. His arms went around her body and he closed his eyes, resting his cheek against the top of her head as she cried. His head roared with unanswered questions and his chest clenched with unfamiliar emotions but he didn't let her go. Even when he had been in the 'solid' world, the only person he'd held to comfort like this had been his mother. Still he didn't let her go. The sensation of another's touch was an odd experience and still he didn't let her go. After a long moment she pulled back slightly but he didn't want to release her. Allowing Matilda to drop her arms from his shoulders he captured her hands in his and simply held them. He held them loosely enough that she could have pulled away had she wanted to, however she relaxed her hands in his and stayed.

"Sorry to barge in like this."

Bastian looked at her for a moment unable to fight the spreading grin.

"There is no need for you to apologise. I find it quite acceptable."

Mattie watched his smile, unable to believe what was happening. To feel him real and solid under her hands filled her with awe. It was like seeing an imaginary being, like a leprechaun, come to life… only better. He felt solid to touch but to look at him was slightly disconcerting. He wasn't solid. He was like a ghost on a TV program. She could see the colour of his clothes and skin but she could also see the darkness behind him.

"Bastian, how is this possible?"

A half smile that was part amusement and part wonder crossed his face.

"I honestly have no idea."

"Well…" She shrugged. She had no idea what to say in a situation like this.

"There is nothing worse than the unknown."

She nodded, seeing anew the wreckage of the plane. "I can only hope that they are alive but Bastian, to see the footage, I mean it's horrible. There is no one who could survive that. If they could it would have to be a miracle."

"Miracles do happen."

"Not ones like this."

"And yet you are standing here with me." Bastian took hold of her free hand. "Perhaps… we should pray."

"Pray?" Mattie was shocked. Praying was outdated in this day and age.

"Yes pray. God provides miracles. We can only ask."

"Um. Okay? I suppose it couldn't hurt."

Bastian closed his eyes and lowered his head. Mattie slowly copied his moves.

"Dear Heavenly Father. I have been away from your presence for a very long time and I ask forgiveness. I have been consumed with my own situation, my own troubles and needs, for far too long; and now I am able to share another's…"

Mattie couldn't help herself. Opening her eyes she glanced at Bastian's face. He sounded so sincere. The only time she had heard people pray had been at her mother's third husband's church and the preacher had prayed standing with his hands in the air and with such a ridiculous over the top sing song voice that it was impossible to take him seriously. She snuck a peek up into the blackness above her. Despite his slightly formal language, Bastian sounded like he was speaking to someone else in the room.

"…we humbly ask for your help in providing a miracle for Matilda and her family. The flying transport fell from the sky and the situation appears dire. If it is in your will we ask that her parents have survived the fall and are whole in body. You are the creator and power over all and we ask for this miracle in the name of your son Jesus Christ. Amen."

She watched as Bastian stayed with his eyes closed and his head bowed for a moment longer, and then slowly lifted his head.

"That's it?" She asked in surprise.

He gave her a curious look.

"I mean don't prayers have to be, you know, longer?"

"Prayers are as long as you need them to be."

"That's the shortest one I have ever heard."

"God is not concerned about the length merely the sincerity."

"Uh… okay. What do you mean about the 'if it is in your will' thing?"

"Exactly as I said."

"Yeah, but what did you mean?"

"God has a plan that is bigger than any one person. If it is not his will for your parents to survive then it is not my place to demand it."

"Then what's the good of asking for a miracle in the first place? Why bother asking for something if it isn't going to happen? That's stupid." Yanking her hands from his she stalked across the room. How could she be so idiotic as to get her hopes up that Bastian would be able to help her?

"We do not know that it will not happen."

"No but it's all at the whim of a God who is so far away and too busy judging with a bunch of rules to care about what we want."

"That is simply not true. Matilda He…"

"Oh what does it matter anyway? It's hopeless."

Bastian reached out and touched her shoulder but she pulled away.

"And who are you to talk? Are you going to tell me that it is God's will that you are here, in this place?"

She waited with her arms folded knowing that he wouldn't be able to give a satisfactory answer.

"I have asked that question many times."

"Yeah? Well it's all a load of crock."

With that she spun on her heel and walked out of his world.

Chapter Twelve

Turning from the mirror Bastian wished he could answer her questions. Right now Matilda wasn't looking for answers, just the hope that her parents could be alive.

Wincing he held the palm of his hand against his forehead. His headaches were getting steadily worse and it was becoming harder to solidify objects. When he had them solidified it took so much more effort to hold them in that state. He hadn't had this trouble since he was first imprisoned here and learning how things worked.

Rubbing at the ache with his fingers he glanced at his arm. To him it looked quite solid but when he'd looked down at Matilda's hands in his he had been shocked to be able to see her hands through his. As she hadn't said anything, he hadn't mentioned it, but it was disconcerting to say the least. He'd felt as substantial as the reflections of the solid Manor.

Dropping his hand he walked slowly to the mirror and unhurriedly reached out to the glass. His fingers touched the usual resistance. The barrier felt as it always did, smooth and cool against his skin. He had always referred to it as glass but he knew from experience that it didn't break, so how did Matilda walk through it as if it were not there?

Walking away from the mirror he returned back to mirrored Manor and stopped short. Unbidden the rooms were fading from sight.

"No." The word burst out as he pushed against the nearest glass as if he could grasp the room and halt its progressive fade. This couldn't be happening. It felt like he'd lost all control of his prison. The ability to view any room at whim and without conscious effort was the only reason he hadn't gone completely mad in the emptiness. It was the only way he could have any kind of human contact. Taking a deep breath he concentrated on keeping the room from fading, the same way he did when he solidified objects. The only result was a greatly increased intensity in his headache followed by the complete darkening of the glass. Shaking in pain and shocked disbelief, Bastian slid to the floor with his hands still on the glass.

"No, please no." He whispered in the darkness.

*　　*　　*　　*　　*

Curled up in an armchair Mattie wrapped her arms around her middle and stared blankly at the empty television screen. There had been no extra news, so she'd turned it off. If only she could turn her emotions off with the same ease as she'd turned off the grating British monotone of the reporter. Wavering between anger, grief and despair she couldn't even cry. Not only was there the fate of her mum and Alex; she also felt as if she'd lost her best friend. She couldn't believe he had so calmly said that if they died then so be it. What the hell was the point of asking for a miracle if you didn't expect it to happen?

Lost in her thoughts she didn't even notice that Stacey had entered the room until she winced in the hash sunlight as the maid opened the curtains.

"Do you have to open the curtains?"

"Oh sorry Miss, uh Mattie, I didn't know you were in here. It's just that the room was so dark and the telly was off. I thought you'd gone with Jonathan."

"Where is Jonathan?" Mattie asked lowering her hand as her eyes became accustomed to the light.

"He said he was sick of doing nothing. I think he went to see Sandy at the…"

"…TV station."

"Yes."

"Yeah okay."

"Look Mattie… sunlight." Stacey said with a ghost of a smile.

Mattie gave a breath of laughter. There was no real amusement but she had to smile. She'd asked two days ago if the sun ever shone in England and of all days, it had chosen today to do so

"It'll do you good to go outside while you have the chance. If you can't do anything but wait you might as well look at the gardens while the sun shines."

"Is that a hint?"

Stacey perched on the couch opposite Mattie.

"When my friend Elizabeth was in a car smash I found the worse thing to do was to sit dwelling on all the 'orrible possibilities. It was better to be doing something, and you might find something to draw or…" She made an 'I don't know' gesture with her hands. "… I don't mean something to take your mind off it, because that's impossible but something to ease the waiting."

Mattie regarded her for a moment then nodded.

"You're probably right."

"I am right."

Uncurling from the chair Mattie went to her room to retrieve her drawing kit and sketch pad. Very deliberately she didn't look at any mirrors along the way. She didn't feel like seeing Bastian at the moment. Descending the stairs to the foyer she stopped abruptly on the last step. Beside the banister was a little half table that held a phone with an answering machine. Unable to move she stood watching the little red blinking light. Her heart pounded as her thoughts skittered like dogs on ice across her mind, each worse than the first. Slowly she sat on the step and hesitantly reached through the banister hovering over the play selection on the LCD screen. Licking her lips and letting her breath out slowly she touched the screen and waited for the electronic female to finish telling her that she had one new message received at 1107pm yesterday. Mattie slumped against the railing. It wouldn't be anything useful. Abruptly she sat bolt upright as she heard Alex's voice from the speaker.

"Hello Jonathan, Mattie. Anyone there? Pick up if you're there…"

To stop herself from picking up the handset, Mattie gripped the wood so hard that her fingers hurt. After all, it wouldn't do any good.

"… I guess not. Anyway, you would not believe what we managed to do."

She closed her eyes as she heard her mum's laughter in the background.

"I bet you they would."

"Perhaps. The thing is, we've managed to miss our flight…"

Mattie blinked slowly then suddenly hit the replay button and listened carefully.

"… we've managed to miss our flight but we were able to book…"

They missed their flight.

Scrabbling at her art kit she grabbed a pencil and quickly scribbled down the rest of Alex's message with the new flight details. Snatching up the phone she hit the number eight speed dial and waited impatiently.

"Greetings lovely. I'm just on the phone at the moment so leave a message."

"Of course you are." Mattie muttered as she listened to the beep. "Jonathan, it's Mattie, they missed their flight. I got the machine message from last night. You didn't check the messages. They missed their flight."

Glancing at her scribble she relayed the flight details and told him to head for the airport. Unable to help herself she leapt to her feet and let out a short scream of pure joy. They were safe and they were alive.

"Mattie, what's the matter?" Stacey came running into the foyer followed by a few of the other maids.

"They missed their flight. They're okay. They missed their flight, they didn't crash, they're alive. They… they missed their flight."

The whole group erupted in cheers and began jumping up and down and hugging each other.

"It's a miracle." Stacey cheered.

Mattie looked at her. Turning she raced down the stairs to the cellar.

Bastian.

Racing around the mirror she called his name.

"Bastian."

Standing in front of it she searched past her grinning reflection for him.

"Bastian. I received your miracle. They didn't get on the plane."

She waited a moment longer.

"Bastian if you don't appear I'm coming in."

She had no idea if she could do it without him directly on the other side, but she was impatient to tell him of the news.

"Fine."

Stepping up to the mirror she placed her hand against the glass. It felt the same as a normal mirror until it rippled like it had before and she automatically stepped back. Grinning again she put her hand to the mirror once more and followed it through. Stumbling to a halt she blinked in the sudden darkness. It hadn't been so dark before. She couldn't see a thing this time. Turning around she was surprised that she couldn't see the chapel. Stepping forward carefully she suddenly found herself back before the altar. She should have brought the torch.

Finding a candle and a handful of matches on a small dusty tray, she grabbed them, hoping that she could take things from her world into his. She reasoned that she could, because otherwise she would enter naked, then she carefully stepped back through the mirror. When the candle and its holder passed easily through the glass with her, she sighed in relief. The candle didn't do much to diminish the darkness. She would be better finding a torch or something. About to blow out the candle and return again through the mirror she heard a sound that sounded suspiciously like a moan.

"Bastian?"

Not knowing what she would encounter, she gingerly stepped towards the sound. The light from the candle was proving to be more of a hindrance then a help. The glow from the flame was too close to be able to see past it and she couldn't direct it to the ground in front of her. Moving the candle as far away from her as possible she shut one eye and squinted into the darkness.

"Bastian?"

Suddenly she saw him and hurried to his side. He was on the ground curled in a foetal position with his hands holding his head.

"Bastian, what's wrong."

He only seemed to notice her when she touched him and flinched under her hand.

"What's the matter?"

His voice was so low she could barely hear him.

"Headache."

"It looks like a doozy." She said relieved it wasn't anything worse. Headaches were normal. "Have you taken any Panadol?"

Gingerly he turned his head to face her. "Panadol?"

"Pain killers, have you taken any pain killers."

He shook his head then immediately winced in pain.

"I'm going to get you some."

Bastian's hand gripped her arm.

"Please don't…"

"Don't? Don't what? You don't want pain killers?"

"Don't go. Please don't go. I… alone"

"Shh, it's okay. I won't go. I'm here.

Moving to the other side of him she shifted to sit cross-legged and urged him to rest his head on her lap. Gently she began to stroke his hair, and after removing the ribbon which held it back, she gradually increased the pressure until she was massaging his head. Whenever her mum had a migraine Mattie would massage until she slept. At first Bastian held himself tense with the pain but after a moment she felt him begin to relax.

"That feels wonderful." He sighed.

"Shh, close your eyes."

"Hmmm."

Mattie almost sighed herself. His hair felt nice under her fingers, soft, long silken strands and she could smell a subtle warm spicy scent that was marvellously pleasant.

"Does that feel any better?" She whispered after a long while. She didn't want to stop but her hands were beginning to get sore.

"A little."

"Try to sleep."

He was silent for a moment. "I can not."

"You will in a moment I promise."

Bastian opened his eyes and turned his head. Her hands stilled as he looked up at her. The glow of the candle turned his eyes such an amazing iridescent green.

"I do not sleep."

She looked down at him in shock. "Ever?"

To her dismay he lifted himself to a sitting position. She would have liked him to stay where he was.

"No. Not for a very long time."

"Do you get tired?"

"No."

"Hungry?"

"No." He smiled. "Nor thirsty, nor cold, nor hot."

"But you do get headaches."

"Yes."

He pushed back the hair that had fallen over his face and she had to smile. His hair was longer than hers.

"Here."

Rising to her knees she shuffled behind him and pulled his hair back retying it with the ribbon. Resting her hands on his shoulders she marvelled that he could feel so real and solid when she knew he was translucent. This time, in the candle light, he didn't appear to be. Acting on impulse she leant forward and kissed his cheek. She could feel the slight roughness of stubble and wondered if he ever needed to shave.

"Thank you."

When she pulled away he tilted his head slightly.

"For what are you thanking me?"

"I got your miracle."

He smiled. "It was not my miracle. It was yours."

"You asked for it. Thank you."

"Thank God, not me."

"Um. I'd rather leave that to you."

He looked away for a moment then nodded. "As you wish."

Mattie was suddenly conscious that she still had her hands on his shoulders and pulled away. "So…"

"Yes?"

"How do you feel?"

It wasn't what she really meant to ask but the way he was looking at her made her forget everything else. She had never been this awkward with him before. Usually the conversation just flowed. Granted it was normally via the tip of a pen.

"Immensely improved, thank you. No headache has ever waned quite so swiftly."

She had become used to reading his unusual way of saying things but to hear it was another thing altogether. It made it so much more obvious that he was from another century.

Suddenly the quiet was penetrated by a piercing reverberation that set her teeth on edge and seemed to rattle right through her. It was agonizing. It sounded several times in succession then, mercifully, all became silent again.

"What the hell was that?" She asked not at all sure she'd regained her equilibrium. She wouldn't say Bastian was unfazed by it, but h did seem to have weathered it better.

"The telephone."

"The telephone? You have a telephone?"

"No. The device is in the solid Manor. Your world."

"And it sounds like *that*?"

"Yes."

"Ugh. How torturous."

"Yes."

"No wonder you get headaches."

She saw his lips twitch and flashed a grin at him. He shook his head and laughed. She almost swooned. His laugh was low and mellow; it reminded her of sun warmed honey oozing off a deep brown honey stick. She could picture it. The sun would be glinting off the stream of slowly melting, pure and sweet amber liquid.

"I have to go. The phone, it might be my Mum or Alex."

Bastian nodded but didn't move.

"I have one small problem."

"What is that?"

"I don't know where to find the mirror, and it's dark."

He merely smiled and gradually the darkness infused into light. She looked behind her and saw rooms of the Manor through hundreds of mirrors. She had assumed his world would be a house like the Manor; not this dark emptiness filled only with mirrors and transparent reflections streaming into the space like so many beams of sunlight.

With a wave of his hand he brought the correct mirror closer to the both of them.

"You could have done that at any time." She accused with a grin.

"Perhaps." He agreed as he stood, then helped her to her feet.

"Thank you. Well I guess I'll see you later."

"You are welcome at any time."

Mattie nodded and put her hand to the mirror. Instead of passing through as she expected her fingers came into sharp contact with the glass.

"Ouch." She said automatically more out of shock than actual pain. Trying again she got the same result. There was a barrier firmly in place. Trying to feel a point of weakness, she pushed against it several times in different areas. There was still no give.

"Bastian, I can't get out."

"Did you previously approach the mirror differently?"

"No. I just walked through it."

"Have you a need to concentrate?"

"No, nothing like that, it just happens."

"What has changed?"

"Nothing." She said with a shrug.

Bastian looked at her then at the mirror several times.

"When you first passed through you were grieving, then angry upon your departure. What was your emotional state as you passed through this time?"

"Um…" She said thinking. "… I was excited…"

"What is you emotional state at this moment?"

"Confused, unsure, I guess."

"Sorrow, anger and excitement are passionate, perplexity not quite so."

"Do you think that has anything to do with it?"

"I honestly do not know. Never have I had someone pass into my prison before."

"So what do I do? Do I have to get angry or something?"

"It should not be difficult."

"What do you mean?"

"You are a woman. Women are highly emotional creatures whose passions are easily…"

Suddenly Bastian stopped speaking and before she realised what he was doing, he had pulled her close and given her a kiss the likes of which she had never known. She'd been kissed before but never like this. His mouth was firm against hers but his lips caressed hers in a way no one else's had ever done.

He didn't try anything with his tongue, merely his lips, and it sent an instantaneous bolt of desire straight through her. As suddenly as he'd bestowed the incredible kiss he ended it, and using her shoulders, turned her to face the mirror.

"Try now."

Baffled she did as he commanded and whacked her hand on the glass.

"Nope, no go." She said shaking her hand as she stood back. He'd kissed her to arouse her anger, no doubt - at his insolence, but it hadn't worked. Though the way it did make her feel would have had the mirror melting into a pool of molten glass if passion was the key. If that kiss was merely to anger her she'd hate to think what the kiss would be like when he meant it. Actually, scrap that, she would *love* to find out what it was like.

Stooping she bent to pick up the candle, more to keep from throwing herself at him than any real need for its tiny flame of light. With kisses like that it was little wonder that the initials in his journal had constantly changed. He was potent. It made her wonder what he was actually like in bed. She felt her cheeks burn and was grateful that he was inspecting the mirror frame rather than looking at her. Despite the free attitude of her friends, she had never found a man who intrigued her enough to take that next step. Now here she was speculating on a gorgeous man's sexual prowess. Not unusual she knew, just not like her.

"As far as I can tell, the mirror is exactly the same as it has always been."

For the first time Mattie felt a flicker of panic. "Does this mean I'm stuck here?"

"I can not say."

Disbelieving she went to knock the glass and stumbled as her hand went right through.

"I didn't do anything different." She said in surprise.

Bastian looked at the mirror then at her. Gently he removed the candle from her hand.

"Try now."

Frowning she put her hand out and touched solid glass. Just as gently he returned the candle. Clicking as to what he was trying to tell her, she put her hand out again and sure enough, it passed through the mirror.

"I can't leave anything behind."

"So it appears."

"Wait here." She said as an impulsive idea came to her.

Stepping through the glass she replaced the candle on the altar and returned to Bastian.

"I want to try something." She said grabbing his hand.

Putting her hand forward she made sure it would pass through the mirror.

"There has to be a reason I can come into your world."

Bastian went very still.

"Could it be so very simple?" He breathed.

"There is only one way to find out." Mattie said as she stepped out of the mirror. She didn't know what to expect, so she took it very slowly. After she entered the chapel completely except for her arm she turned to face him. He took a step forward and she held her breath. Abruptly her arm was jerked as though on a chain. Bastian had walked into the mirror. It didn't work. Hastily she returned to his side.

"I'm sorry." She said.

"There is no reason for you to be. If it was not tried, how were we to know it would not work?"

"Yeah, I suppose so." She said sadly. She had been hoping so much that it would work, and the disappointment would be worse for Bastian.

"You should go Matilda. The arrival of you parents is imminent."

"Are you sure?"

"You said so yourself."

"I didn't mean…"

"Go." He said softly.

Chapter Thirteen

The call ended up being a girl named Wynona calling for Jonathan and had nothing to do with Alex or her mum. They arrived with Jonathan an hour and a half later and she had never thought it possible for four people to make so much noise. They came in bearing gifts of Chinese takeaway which they ended up eating in the kitchen rather than in the dining room. Her mum's mane of blond hair had more honey tones than she could recall but other than that she was exactly how Mattie remembered her. She nearly burst into tears of relief the moment she saw her.

"Oh it's good to see you again." Crystal said, grabbing Mattie into a bone crushing hug. It was like being small all over again. Mattie hugged her back, more glad than she could say.

"You don't look any different, except - have you lost weight?" Crystal's eyebrow went up as she asked.

"A little."

"I knew it."

"Mattie."

"Alex. It's nice to finally meet you." She greeted reaching out to shake his hand only to find herself enfolded in another hug.

"You are family now. There is no need to be so formal."

Alex looked exactly like his photos except he was more relaxed.

"I feel like I already know you from all the phone conversations and everything your mother has told me."

"Nothing good, I hope." Mattie teased.

"Of course not. He would never have wanted to meet you otherwise."

"Did you really draw a mural depicting your graduating class of high school on the wall of the school in the dark of night before graduation day?"

"Yes."

"You did what?" Jonathan demanded, dumping utensils on the table.

"See I told you." Crystal gloated.

"And you didn't get into trouble for it."

"No."

"Unbelievable."

"Did she also tell you it was done in chalk so it would wash off?" Mattie said as she accepted the box of noodles from Alex.

"Spoil sport. Don't ruin a perfectly good story with facts."

"Says the historian." Alex teased.

"Well I can't have him thinking I have a graffiti habit, he'll never let me out of my room."

"Oh I don't know. Some of the walls around here could do with a bit of sprucing up."

"I like them the way they are." Alex said with a pointed look in Jonathan's direction.

"Ahh, do I detect a childhood prank in that comment?" Crystal teased her new husband.

"No."

"I'm just saying that this place needs to be brought properly into the twenty-first century." Jonathan licked his fingers and didn't meet his father's gaze.

"Kicking and screaming. It has an old fashioned charm that lends a perfect ambiance. You would lose it if you tried to modernise it much more. It fits with the solid Manor."

"The what?" Jonathan asked.

"The so…" It was only then that Mattie realised her slip. "The Manor, you know, the place attached… that-a-way that you lead tours through."

"Why did you call it that? The solid Manor?"

"Umm." She couldn't think of a single excuse. "I have no idea."

"I think I know what you mean." Crystal said.

"You do?"

"Yes. A lot of hard work and effort has gone into the Manor to make it as historically accurate as possible. Sometimes it feels like you've stepped back in time and can hold history in your hand."

"Well Mattie would know." Jonathan grinned.

Mattie looked at him suspiciously. "What do you mean?"

"I mean the amount of time you've spent researching my family history. By now, you should know them all chronologically, along with their birthdays, their favourite colours, and what they liked to drink for a nightcap!"

She knew Bastian's, red and malt whisky for the nightcap.

"Mattie? I don't believe it." Crystal laughed pinching a water chestnut from Mattie's plate. "Unless it had something to do with influences on art, then perhaps, but normal history, not a chance."

"It's true." Jonathan insisted.

"Who are you and what have you done with my daughter?"

"Ahh, another has fallen into its grasp." Alex spoke as if stating the obvious. "The family curse. You are trying to figure it out?"

"Well yes."

"Join the club. I've been trying to figure it out since I was old enough to understand words."

"If anyone can figure it out it'll be Mattie. You're good at puzzles." Crystal laughed.

"Talking about puzzles Dad, did I tell you that she figured that puzzle box overnight?"

"Puzzle box?" Alex asked.

"Yeah. You know, the one Mother found."

"You solved that in one night?"

"In about two hours actually."

"How did you manage that? Jonathan's been attempting that box for years."

"I just needed to look at it from a different angle and it simply fell into place." Mattie hedged.

"She found some things in it: a mirror, some jewellery and an old book."

"You did?"

Mattie nodded slowly, wishing that Jonathan had kept quiet, but then he wouldn't have thought he needed to.

"You should have Anderson appraise them."

"Yeah I know." Jonathan said. "Have we actually done that yet?"

"Uh… no, not yet. I'll take them tomorrow." Mattie promised slowly. She didn't want to lose Bastian's diary.

"I said she could keep whatever she found."

"I see, let's hope you won't have to go back on your word. So what conclusions have you drawn?" Alex asked.

"About the puzzle box?"

"About the curse."

Mattie shot a quick look at Jonathan and he smiled slowly, raised an eyebrow, but didn't say anything.

"I think the curse has already been cast and that the rhyme clues as to how you can break it."

"Except she's come up with a different rhyme." Jonathan put in.

"What is it?"

Mattie recited both verses and Alex looked thoughtful.

"Where did you find that?"

"Somewhere in the Manor."

"I've never heard of it, the rhyme I mean. It sounds better than the one we use mind, we may have to steal it."

Mattie just shrugged. "You know, it could be the real one."

Chewing a piece of pork she listened to their laughter and breathed a sigh of relief when Jonathan asked them about their honeymoon. The topics of conversation stayed on safe ground as they finished their food and moved into the games room, where Mattie and Crystal thrashed the men in a game of ping-pong.

"Oh that reminds me Dad, I found someone who can do my portrait."

"How much would I win if I wagered the artist is a woman?"

"All of it." Jonathan grinned. "Mattie, show Dad that drawing you did of me."

"What ever happened to the word please?" Mattie demanded with a smile even though her stomach did its familiar clench at the thought of someone viewing an unfinished drawing.

Jonathan grinned and fell theatrically to his knees. "Mattie, oh Great and esteemed artist with no peer, will you submit to your humble servant's unworthy request and retrieve the highly prized and oh so lovingly created masterpiece that you so tender-heartedly fashioned to capture and display your humble and simple servant."

"Simple is right." Mattie laughed. "You're an utter nutter."

"I can't help it. You bring out my better qualities oh Great One." Jonathan enthused.

"Fine. I'll get it."

"Many thanks Mistress I am in your debt."

"Yeah right." Mattie laughed shaking her head. Taking the steps two at a time she wondered how she had ever thought that Jonathan would be a boring old Pom. He couldn't be that even if he tried. He never took anything seriously enough.

Flipping to the correct page she held the sketch pad to her chest as she re-entered the games room.

"Now bear in mind that it isn't quite finished." She warned.

Alex nodded and she hesitantly handed it over. He let out a low whistle and inspected it more closely.

"Mattie this is better than good, this is fantastic."

"Thank you." Mattie accepted self-consciously.

"I mean it."

"May I see?" Crystal asked.

"You might as well."

"I knew that you could draw but this is amazing. It's almost as if you copied a black and white photo, only improved." Alex continued as he passed it over.

"Well I didn't."

"I didn't mean to say that you did. You've captured Jonathan magnificently. We couldn't use that as a portrait though."

"Why not?" Jonathan demanded.

"It would put the other portraits to shame."

Mattie smiled self-consciously at his praise. As much as she liked the idea that people admired her work it felt strange when people gushed about it in front of her.

"Well, well, well Mattie. Who's the spunk?"

Mattie looked over as her mum turned the pad so she could see the drawing. It was Bastian.

"Mum, you know better than to look though my sketches." Mattie protested as she made a grab for her book, but Jonathan reached it first.

"Oh come on Mattie. It's a finished picture." Crystal defended.

"So?"

"So I want to know who the model is."

"Nobody."

"He doesn't look like a 'nobody' to me. He looks like a very attractive somebody."

"He's nobody you'd know." She tried to take the book from Jonathan, but he held it out of reach. "Please may I have my book Jonathan?"

"As soon as you answer Crystal's question because I'm intrigued. You never told me you'd met anyone here." He said with a small frown.

"Who said I met him here?"

"The order of your drawings does. This is drawn after mine right?"

"So?"

"So, it means you drew him after you drew me."

"Not necessarily. Oh fine." She said when Jonathan wouldn't relinquish the book. "He's one of your ancestors, Sebastian Ashcombe. I copied his portrait and went on from there. Now can I have my book back?"

"Was that so hard?" Jonathan asked as he handed it back. "And it explains why you've drawn him the way you did."

Mattie snapped the book shut and glared at him. The drawing was of Bastian writing in their book at the dresser. She'd drawn enough of her side of the room to show that he was in the mirror while there was no one seated in front of it to cause the reflection.

"How is that?" Crystal asked.

"A conversation we had about one of Mattie's curse theories and mirrors. She thinks that our, however many greats it is, Uncle Sebastian, who disappeared in 1869, is trapped behind a mirror and the curse is the way to free him."

"You said it was plausible." Mattie defended.

"I said I was reserving judgement."

"It makes sense." Alex mused. "The curse does mention a mirror, and with the Ashcombe history with mirrors I wouldn't be surprised."

"Ha. Thank you Alex."

Crystal laughed and they all turned to her.

"The way you pair are acting I could swear you really were siblings."

"Since you got married, we really are." Mattie pointed out.

"But we're not siblings by blood so it doesn't make it real."

"Even if a cubic zirconia is a fake diamond, it's a real cubic zirconia."

"What has that got to do with anything?"

"Well now Mum and Alex are married then we are real siblings…"

"Ahh, but it doesn't make us… authentic siblings, because diamonds are authentic, cubic zirconias are…"

"Enough." Alex said shaking his head. "Now if you don't mind I am going to bed. I'm exhausted and jet lagged. Mattie it was nice to meet you and hopefully I'll be better company tomorrow. Goodnight and don't be up all night arguing with Jonathan."

"I won't I promise."

"I'm with him." Crystal said as she kissed Mattie's cheek. "Goodnight."

"Night." Both Mattie and Jonathan chorused.

"So…"Jonathan said after they left. "You want to do something?"

"Nah, I think I'll join the band wagon and head for bed."

"You want some company."

Mattie stared at him, unamused. "No thank you."

Chapter Fourteen

The shading wasn't right. Closing her eyes Mattie tried to visualise Bastian in the candle light after she'd massaged his head. She could clearly see the way his hair had fallen forward, and the glint of light in his green eyes, she just couldn't seem to reproduce it adequately.

A movement at the door attracted her attention and she looked up as Crystal came into the sun room.

"So this is where you've been hiding. I thought you may have gone into Dunmore to do some shopping or something."

Mattie gave her a look. They both knew she wasn't much of a shopper, though she wasn't adverse to a good art or bookshop.

"I did say 'or something'. Come into my study, I've got something to show you."

"What is it?"

"The curse poem you recited last night. I remembered this morning that I have read it before."

"You have?"

"Yes, come on."

She leapt from the bench, nearly tipping her art kit from her lap in her haste, and followed her mother with curiosity burning. Crystal led the way into the archive office, which, particularly when compared to the Manor, was stark and modern. White lights and metal furnishings. Entering the environmentally controlled restoration room Mattie sat on the tall stool her mum indicated.

"This is your study?"

"I know, fantastic isn't it?"

Mattie raised her eyebrows but didn't comment.

"Hopefully I won't bore you with too much history but I thought this might interest you." She placed a pile of notebooks between them and flicked open the first one. "Are you aware of Natalia Ashcombe ?"

"No."

"She was the wife of Ernest Ashcombe who…"

"Was the first Ashcombe at the Manor after the King gave him the land."

Crystal looked at Mattie in surprise. "I am impressed."

"Some stuff stays in here you know." Mattie said tapping her head.

"Now Natalia is the whole reason I came to England to work. Alex had heard of my work restoring the manuscripts in Canberra and thought that I might be able to restore some manuscripts that were found in a hidden compartment of a desk that was being restored. The manuscripts turned out to be diaries kept by none other than Natalia Ashcombe, some dating back to her childhood in Russia…"

"People seemed to do that on a regular basis in the old days. Keep diaries."

"This was a time before film, cameras and computers. They had to capture their memories somehow, of which I am glad. Anyway the reason I didn't twig right away about your poem is because Natalia was Russian therefore as, you might have guessed, she kept her diary in Russian. As Russian is not one of the languages I am fluent in translating, it has been slow going, and at the moment I am concentrating more on translating than actually reading the diary, but the poem I remembered. Now the actual manuscripts are too delicate too handle often so these are my notes. See…”

Mattie read the page her mum handed her and sure enough there was the curse in amongst all the rest of the notes.

“The main reason that I recalled it was the fact that it is the only thing I’ve read in Natalia’s diaries so far, and she is forty at this time, that is written in English, not Russian.”

“But that would mean the curse has been around for hundreds of years.”

“Since May 1540 at least.”

“That’s centuries before it was written into the Ashcombe history books.”

“I know. Mattie, where did you find the poem?”

“On the front of a mirror.” She replied absently trying to wrap her head around the idea. How did the gypsy nurse fit into it if the curse was that old?

“Which mirror?”

Mattie looked up as her mother grabbed her hand excitedly.

“I… can’t remember.” She lied. She couldn’t give it away; it was her connection with Bastian.

“You can’t remember?”

“It was one of the many.” Mattie shrugged.

"Bugger." Crystal tapped the metal bench-top a moment. "Can you remember what it looked like?"

"Um… it was big."

"How big?"

"Bigger than a person."

"What was it made of?"

"Glass." Mattie said with a frown. "What else are mirrors made off?"

"I mean the frame. What did it look like?"

"Does it matter?"

"I have a comprehensive record of mirrors that have entered Ashcombe hands since 1529, as comprehensive as one can get when it comes to history anyway. You see Natalia was the daughter of Victor Dolembo who came from Russia in 1509. He was a mirror maker and began a company of mirror and glass makers which as it so happens has made all the Ashcombe mirrors since the first given by Ernest to Natalia on their wedding day. It was Natalia who drew up the contract between her father's company and the Ashcombes that Zerkano would make all the mirrors for as long as both the Ashcombes and Zerkano existed. That mirror could be a connection to the curse that could provide a vital clue. You see you are not the only one who is intrigued by the Ashcombe curse." Crystal grinned, her eyes flashing in the way they did when she was fired up on some piece of history. "Now that mirror, anything you can remember, anything at all, you never know. Major discoveries have been known to hinge on the seemingly most insignificant of details."

"Um…" She had to admit that for the first time her mum's passion and thirst for a hint of history was infectious. She could pick her mother's brain on this, but she would have to be careful not to give Bastian away. "It was big, in the shape of a shield only with rounded edges at the top and square at the bottom. It had a raised etching of the Ashcombe crest on the back about three quarters of the way up."

Crystal frowned and wheeled her stool to a computer at the side of the room. "I don't recognise the description but that doesn't mean anything. The Ashcombes have more than eighty-five mirrors around the place and several more that I'm sure have been broken over the years."

"This one wasn't broken."

Crystal navigated the programs until she came to the one she needed then punched the keys. "I'm asking it to search for all the mirrors with the Ashcombe crest."

She waited a moment watching the screen while Mattie wheeled her own stool closer to the computer.

"Seven. Well that does narrow it down a bit. Now this side of the screen shows the design of the mirror, some with pictures but the older ones with design sketches. That should pique your interest." Crystal said with a smile. "The other side gives dimensions and dates and this bit…" She said pointing "…is my favourite, that is where the research and history of the mirrors have been typed. Very interesting. Take this one for example… Design drawings were done by Percival Ashcombe, 1840 to 1903. The mirror was to be the bridal present to

Penelope Ashcombe (nee Cranston) but by all accounts was never given to her as her husband Sebastian Ashcombe 1836 to 1869 disappeared on their wedding night. The whereabouts of the mirror is unknown, and speculation is that it may have disappeared with him… Sebastian Ashcombe, that's your guy isn't it? Oh, Mattie can you imagine what it would be like to find that mirror? Look at the design."

It wasn't the design of Sebastian's mirror that held her in stunned silence, it was the revelation that he was married. She had assumed he had disappeared into the mirror on his wedding day, before the ceremony. He was married… widowed. Mrs Penelope Ashcombe was long dead.

"Here…" Crystal pushed away from the computer. "…flick through those and see if any of them match the mirror you saw. Are you okay?"

"Yeah… yeah. Thanks."

She took her mum's place and scrolled through the records.

"This one."

Crystal resumed her place in front of the computer and read the information.

"Mattie, are you sure?"

"Yes."

"And it wasn't broken?"

"No, why?"

"It says here that this mirror was destroyed by Annette Ashcombe in 1564. Mattie this was the mirror given by Ernest to Natalia on their wedding day."

"Why would it say that Annette destroyed it?"

"According to what I could find on Annette, she didn't exactly have it all together. She went cuckoo after Walter disappeared. Even after the local authorities called off the investigation she tried to look for him on her own. She would disappear for days on end and blamed her Mother-in-law for Walter's disappearance. I suppose she destroyed the mirror to spite Natalia, but it may be that she didn't destroy it after all, if this is truly the mirror you've found."

"I thought Walter disappeared in 1553."

"He did."

"Then why wait eleven years to …" Mattie frowned then trailed off as she saw the mirror in her mind's eye.

"What are you thinking?"

"She disappeared for days on end?"

"So the records say."

"Do you know if she continued to disappear for days on end after 15… what was it… 1563? When she supposedly destroyed the mirror."

"64. I don't know. I don't think it mentions anything."

"She knew… and he must have turned forty-four. In 1564, he turned forty-four. She couldn't… he was gone."

"What are you talking about?"

"Mum did Walter turn forty-four in 1564?"

Crystal wheeled over to her note books on the table and began flicking through them.

"Born 1520, so… yes. Why is that important?"

"Ashcombe man in reflection thou will stay, hidden in sight thy debt to pay, until four and forty natal day, thy existence ends and thy time fades away." Mattie recited. "Can I read what you've translated from Natalia's diaries?" She asked wheeling her own stool across the room.

"Sure, be my guest."

"Can I take them away with me?"

Crystal smiled. "I never thought I'd live to see the day when you'd be interested in history."

"Ta da." Mattie posed in jest.

"Sure you can. You can take these notebooks, just not this one; I'm still working on it."

"Is it the one with the curse?"

"No, that's this one."

"Thanks."

Chapter Fifteen

"Nothing. You?" Matilda closed the notebook she'd been reading and took the next one.

"I've found naught of the curse yet." Bastian replied keeping his eyes on the notebook he'd selected.

They sat on the solidified reflection of her bed. He'd tried to solidify two chairs at the same time several weeks ago, and failed. Matilda had hit the floor hard, or for what passed as a floor in here, and insisted that he not try again. The headache from that had lasted nearly a full day and he suspected she had sustained some nasty bruises even though she had waved away his concern.

"She appears to have been most vigilant regarding her husband's activities." He commented.

"Yeah, she does seem to control him. Every second entry has something about it… He will not defy me… I will have his obedience… He will listen and do as I say… He will not say no to me, I will not have it… I will make him sorry for this… I wonder what his diaries would have said about it."

Bastian's brow rose but he kept his attention on the book. He doubted from Ernest's dealings with King Henry that the man was weak willed, so he deduced that the marriage had been far from easy. Under the pretence of reading the translation of Natalia's diary he surreptitiously watched Matilda out of the corner of his eye. Much as he was eager to find the solution of the curse he found his attention wandering. She sat against the pillows with the diary translation in her left hand and a pen in her right hovering over a notepad on her lap; she appeared completely comfortable and at ease while he was extraordinarily conscious of how close her stocking sheathed foot was to his leg.

Perhaps it was due to her astounding ability to enter his prison or perhaps because over the last three weeks she had spent multiple hours in here with him, but he had come to crave her company and greedily devoured every minute of her presence. Mostly they pored over the diaries and other reference materials she brought in with her, but sometimes they shared conversations which, while highlighting very clearly the differences between their culture and centuries, he had begun to crave. Despite her self-deprecating humour and shocking etiquette, she had an engaging intellect and no fear of displaying it.

"Hey, listen to this." Matilda interrupted his thoughts as she began to read. " '…It is doubtful that tonight I will sleep. The ball was a success. Tonight the erosardoris was prepared and ready for use. Grandmother has taught me well but warns that it must be used sparingly as the results will be adverse and obsessive. I believe I was careful. All that is left to do now… is to wait. All will be well I know it…' Mum has written the word 'erosardoris' in the margin with question marks all around it and the notation 'not Russian'.

The rest of the entry is only about the fact that she danced with Mr. Ashcombe, Ernest presumably, several times during the King's ball, and that tonight will be the beginning of the rest of her life. She is fairly cocky about it… 'I will become more than even my mother dreamed. His is a favourite of the King of this country and I will be a favourite, no not a favourite, the favourite of his. He will be mine…' " Matilda looked up at him. "This appears to be the actual first meeting between the two of them and she's sure he'll marry her. I mean she ends up being right and all, but crikey talk about being sure of your sex appeal."

If Bastian had been sipping a drink he would have choked. As it was he stared at Matilda in shock. He was becoming used to the liberal way she spoke but it was still indecent to hear a woman speak of such things so candidly.

"If she was all that, no wonder he was under her thumb. She was obviously very much in control."

A sudden memory came to him. "How is the word spelt?"

"Which word?"

"The item she is to use sparingly."

She spelt it out.

"I have seen it several times, though not in the diary entries before she is married. Those after her marriage are a different story."

"It is?" Matilda asked "I didn't realise you'd read the later ones."

"I have the spare time."

"When?"

"While you slumber."

"Oh that's right. You don't sleep."

He smiled faintly. "I must say that it is easier to read while you are here."

"Really?"

"Yes, the headache I receive while solidifying is not conducive to the ease of reading. The bed is one item, but trying to read while solidifying a chair, table, notebook, pen and diary notes is altogether another thing."

"I suppose it would be."

For some reason he felt a flutter of optimism at the way her smile faltered just a little.

"I enjoy your company also Matilda." He tested quietly.

"I'm sure you do. You'd enjoy the boogie man if he could keep you company."

"I doubt he would be quite as beautiful."

"I don't know. Stale bread is a gourmet meal to a man who is starving."

He gave a faint smile at her self-deprecation

"What's that smile for?"

"You do yourself an injustice to say such things."

"Not when it's the truth. As I said to Jonathan, I've done too many self-portraits."

"Then it is a good thing that beauty is in the eye of the beholder. There is no need that you should find yourself beautiful; only be aware that others do."

"I don't need that."

"Another good thing, otherwise you would be conceited and dull."

Matilda stared at him a moment then laughed. "I bet you say that to all the girls."

"No." He said seriously then, seeing the proof of her embarrassment stain her cheeks, winked. "At least not in a long while."

She laughed again and fanned herself with her hand. "You don't need to practice your flattery. You're already far too good at it as it is."

Biting his tongue against the desire to reassure her that he did not speak to flatter, he picked up his own notepad which Matilda had provided. He did not wish to frighten her into leaving.

"Natalia writes of the erosardoris as if it is a recipe. It is used, as you have said, in careful doses, loses its effect over a period of continued use and takes a month to prepare." He said consulting his notes.

Matilda frowned and chewed the lid at the end of her pen. "Hang on."

She flipped the page of the diary entries and ran her finger down the writing. After several pages she chewed the pen lid again while she read then consulted her own notes.

"Bloody hell, it sounds like she's controlling him with it, like it's a drug or something."

Suddenly part of the word jumped out at him. " 'Eros', it is Greek for love, particularly the love between a man and a woman. Erosardoris, and ardour means passion. Love-passion."

They stared at each other in shared surprise.

"A love potion. Do you reckon she was a witch?" Matilda asked breaking the silence.

Bastian felt an involuntary shudder ripple down his spine as verses from Leviticus passed through his mind. He believed in God, therefore believed that Lucifer existed. It would be reasonable that those who worshipped him also existed, but to have one in his own bloodline was abhorrent.

The silence which followed Matilda's words was unexpectedly ended by a piping sound. He looked up in surprise as she checked her time piece then covered it with her hand, causing the sound to cease.

"I have to go."

He nodded absently. "Yes, your ball."

"Nothing so fancy. It will be mostly Jonathan's friends and some people that Alex and Mum know. It's a Christmas thing."

Helping her to collect the books and other materials he made certain that she'd left nothing behind as she replaced her shoes upon her feet and walked her to the mirror.

"Bastian?"

"Yes?"

"Are you okay? You've gone quiet."

"Pensive. As enlightening as it is to discover the 'whom' it does not help with the 'how', or the 'how to'

She studied him for a moment and he managed a smile, which she did not return.

"Okay. We'll work this out, alright?"

When he nodded she pressed her lips against his cheek. He was tempted to move just that fraction needed to bring her lips to his but he did not. He would have done so while he was on the other side of the mirror, he knew, but somewhere along the way

she had become more than his conquests had ever
been. She had become his confidante and friend; her
trust and respect were worth more than a stolen kiss.
Watching her pass through the glass, he moved away
from the foul thing, glad that he need not 'appear'
before the mirror for her to leave. He re-solidified her
bed, and lying upon it he tried to sort through this
new revelation while he waited for her to reappear in
her bedroom. She placed the books on the dresser,
spines facing the mirror so he could make his
selection with ease. Then she covered the mirror in
the bathroom with a towel. There was not much he
could do to alter the past, so he refused to dwell on
what his Grandmother - sixteen generations before
him - had been, and tried to concentrate on what to do
regarding how it affected him now.

Chapter Sixteen

They were running out of time. She knew Bastian was working on the assumption that they had just over two months left to find a way to break the curse and she hadn't told him otherwise. He didn't know that she only had two weeks left in England.

He was right though, knowing who had cursed the family didn't help.

"You seem preoccupied."

Mattie looked up as Tiffany sat beside her on the couch. The older generation were in the dining room while Jonathan's friends had gravitated to the games room. Her mum had shooed her along with the 'young people' so she had found a quiet corner out of the way to be alone with her thoughts.

"Pensive."

"What?"

She shook her head. "Never mind."

"I hear you drew Jonathan's portrait."

"Where did you hear that?"

"Jonathan."

"Big mouth."

"So it's true?"

"Yes."

"Cool. So…how does it feel to be an Ashcombe?"

"I'm not."

"By marriage you are."

"Not my marriage."

"Ahh, it's not that bad, practically all of Dunmore is related somewhere along the way."

Mattie finally looked at her. "Really?"

"Yeah, take me for instance. One of my Great-great, however many Aunts married one of the Ashcombes. And my family has run alongside them until 1917."

"What happened in 1917?"

"The Russian revolution. Have you heard of Zerkano?"

Tiffany had her attention.

"It's Russian for mirror and the name of the mirror makers for the Ashcombe family."

"I'm impressed. You have been busy… unless you've been on one of the tours."

"I have been on the tour, but I don't remember Zerkano from there."

"That's alright; there is a lot of information to take in on one of those. I'm sure it comes as no surprise to hear that when we did local history at school, Jonathan got top marks… and the only class he did so"

"I can imagine."

"Anyway, my Great-grandfather's cousin was the last to run the business. It was somehow commissioned from somewhere in Russia and the support was yanked because of the revolution, it didn't survive even with the Ashcombes as their biggest client."

"So you'd know a bit about the history of the mirrors of Ashcombe."

"Me? No, not much. Not all that interested to tell you the truth, though my mum reckons that the Ashcombe line will cease with Jonathan."

"Why?"

"Well look at him." Tiffany said indicating with her glass to where Jonathan was flirting with a group of women. "No brothers or sisters, by blood I mean, and he's not the sort to settle down in a hurry. I pity him. Imagine having that sort of responsibility on your shoulders. Ugh, he can have it."

"You wouldn't want to marry him?"

"I'd marry him in a flash, can you image the doors that would open for an Ashcombe around here? but as I said, he's not the sort to settle down."

"You'd have to have kids, male kids to keep the line going." Mattie said raising her eyebrows. She didn't peg Tiffany as the mothering sort.

"Yeah… there is that. But that wouldn't be the worse part."

"What's the worst part?"

"If I married him I'd want him to stop fooling around and I'm afraid that would be similar to asking the tide to stop." Tiffany took the last mouthful of her drink. "How many of them do you think would hang around if Jonathan wasn't who he was, you know, money and name and all that?"

Mattie shrugged. "Would you?"

"The pathetic thing is yes, I know I would."

"Why is that pathetic?"

"Because I know he doesn't feel the same way." It was her turn to shrug. "To him, I'm just one of the many. It is simply the Ashcombe way."

"The Ashcombe way?"

"They are far too good in bed and they don't like staying in the same one for long."

That caused Mattie to jerk upright. "Surely not all of them, I mean Alex…"

"Nah, your mum's safe with Jonathan's father. He might have been wild in his youth, but he settled down. It's the others that played the bed hop."

Mattie studied Tiffany a moment. "Why are you telling me this?"

"Because of all the women in this room you are the only one who is not my competition."

"Believe me, Jonathan is all yours."

"That's just it. I wish he actually was."

"Do you love him?"

Tiffany slowly looked across the room to where Jonathan was leaning over a girl showing her how to sink the pool ball.

"Since the day he rescued me from a tree when I was six. You know, my mum has this crazy idea about a love potion, some secret family recipe. Sometimes I wish I had some of that to make him notice me and me alone."

For a moment Mattie was speechless. "That sort of stuff will just get you into trouble. Besides then you'll always wonder and wish he loved you for you and not because you took away his free will to decide."

"When you put it that way, it does sound pretty awful." Tiffany stared at her empty wine glass. She sighed then brightened. "Well anyway, enough of this little heart-to-heart, it's too morose for me. I suppose I'll have to ask Jonathan for more wine."

"The bar's open to everyone."

"Hmm, I know, but I've just had the last of the Cabernet Sauvignon and I don't like to mix drinks, it gives me an awful headache."

"I can get it."

"Have you seen the size of the Ashcombe cellar? You'll get lost."

"She'll be right, I've got the hang of it. Unless your real intention is to pry Jonathan away from what's-her-name."

"Now that's an idea. Wish me luck."

Mattie smiled. "Good luck."

Finishing her own drink Mattie made an unnoticed exit to her room. Tiffany's little 'heart-to-heart' as she'd called it, had her mind racing. She felt as if she was on the verge of a break through with the curse, if only she could get the pieces to fit. Passing by the dresser she took the notebook with the curse written in the diary entry and lay on the sofa with it and her own notebook.

It was a punishment, that bit was clear enough. Punishment for what? Mattie flicked back a few entries and began reading.

Nothing. All it said was that she was concerned that her potion was failing to work. What was she missing? Closing her eyes she put her head back on the cushions.

Hidden in sight, thy debt to pay… thy vanity keep thee… thy debt to pay… vanity…mirrors… vanity thy name is woman… Ashcombe man…

vanity is mostly associated with woman… I'm just one of the many… why vanity? …debt to pay… punishment… Natalia's love potion had ceased to work… It is simply the Ashcombe way… vanity keep thee…

Suddenly Mattie sat up, the notebook landing unnoticed on the floor.

"Bloody hell, talk about a woman scorned."

Suddenly another thought ran through her head and she froze in shock for a moment. As much as she didn't want to believe it, it had to be true for her theory to be correct.

Leaving her room she headed for the chapel.

Taking a slow breath she watched the glass ripple then slowly stepped through the mirror. He was sitting on the reflection of her bed reading one of the notebook diaries.

"Bastian?"

Bastian started then smiled when he saw her.

"How was your evening?"

"Ok, um… I need to ask you about Penelope."

"Penelope?"

"I…" She took another deep breath, this was harder than she thought it would be, but she couldn't ask him via their book. "I have a theory that the 'vanity' in the curse has nothing to do with mirrors, but rather with… wo… womanising. Bastian did you… did you cheat on your wife?" She stopped, not able to look at him.

Her heart thudded in her chest as she waited. Never in her life had she so wanted to be wrong.

His voice was so low she almost missed his response. "Yes."

She felt as if he had kicked her in the guts. She wanted to know why, she wanted him to defend himself, to give a reason, an excuse… anything.

He remained silent.

Without a word she turned and left the mirror world. Slumping against the altar she put her head in her hands.

"Oh damn." She whispered at her own swirling thoughts, then slammed her fist on the altar top. She wanted to lash out at him, to hit him, to hurt him. How dare he do something like that… to his wife… on their wedding day?

Battered by her roiling emotions she exited the chapel and ascended the stairs.

"Mattie."

She jumped a mile. "Jonathan."

"What are you doing down here?"

"Um…Tiffany wanted some wine."

Thankfully she was near the door of the cellar and nowhere near the entrance to the chapel.

"Just like her, she asked me to get some as well."

"I thought that was over an hour ago."

"It was. This time I'm taking more than two bottles."

Jonathan took a second look at her and reached over to her shoulder.

"Hey Mattie… are you okay, you look as if you're about to cry."

"I'm fine." She said quickly.

"Why don't I believe you?"

"I don't know, but I'm fine really."

"You say that a couple more times and you'll believe it. What's the matter Mattie, and I'm serious. You haven't been yourself lately. You're spaced out and you disappear for hours."

She could only look at him, she hadn't realised her absences had been noticed. She'd only gone to Bastian late at night or early in the morning with the very occasional visit during the day when everyone else had gone out or were busy.

"Come here."

He wrapped his arms around her and without thinking she automatically hugged him back. She only realised how he took it when he held her closer and lowered his head to hers. For a moment she stood in shock then galvanised into action when she felt his tongue. Rearing back she pulled away and slapped him as hard as she could.

"Damn Mattie, what the hell was that for?"

"You know damn well what that was for." She blazed. "You think a woman, any woman, is yours for the taking, even your own sister. Pull your head in Jonathan. Stop thinking with your pants for God's sake and just start thinking. You have to marry and do not think that you will continue to behave like this after you do. You won't be able to. You think the Ashcombe curse is a joke? Just don't. Bloody hell Jonathan you're next and only you can save yourself."

She couldn't help it. She burst into tears and ran uncaringly to her room where she locked her door and flung herself on her bed.

For all his sophistication, manners and chivalry he was exactly like any man in today's world. He was just like Jonathan, and the mirror had Jonathan's name on it.

Chapter Seventeen

"Come on you, we are going for a drive."

Mattie looked up from the Tangram puzzle to where her mum stood in the doorway. "Why?"

"Because I said so, come on."

"What for?"

"To get you out of the house."

"I don't need to get out of the house."

"Oh you most definitely do."

Mattie sighed and looked back at the uncooperative puzzle. Crystal sat in the chair beside her.

"Tell me what's going on."

"Nothing."

Crystal placed her hand over Mattie's so she couldn't pick up the next piece.

"You have been moody, snapping at everyone and not talking to anyone. This is not like you and I want to know what's going on."

"You wouldn't believe me if I told you."

"Try me."

Mattie stared at the puzzle piece just out of reach.

"Is it boy trouble?"

"Yeah, you could say that."

"What did he do?"

Mattie considered her options. Her mum was an historian, but that didn't guarantee that she would believe her… but she did have to tell someone or she would go crazy.

"Cheated on his wife."

Crystal drew in a sharp breath. "Are you involved with a married man?"

"No, no nothing like that. He's widowed… and I wouldn't exactly say I was involved, well not in the way you might think."

"Have I met him?"

"In a way."

"That's very evasive. Is he someone I would disapprove of, is that why all this secrecy?"

"I don't think so."

"Then what's the matter with him, is he considerably older than you or something?"

"Yes, yes he is, considerably older."

"Twenty years?"

"Over one hundred and fifty."

"What?"

"Mum, is there somewhere we can talk alone?"

Crystal stared at her for a moment. "My study?"

"Okay, I'll meet you there shortly; I need to grab some things first."

An hour later, Mattie sat opposite her mum waiting for her to say something. Silently Crystal ran her hand over Bastian's things, his mirror, the jewellery and his diary pausing to pick up and scan their shared book once more.

"This is… I'm not sure what to make of it."

"Do you believe me?"

"Coming from anyone else I'd be sceptical, but despite the kooky friends you hang around with I've never known you to lie or play practical jokes."

"It's not a joke."

Mattie held her breath, she could understand if her mum didn't believe her, but she needed her to believe.

"If what you say is true…"

"It is."

"Then I'd suggest you give the poor guy a break. He's been paying for his adultery for a very long time."

Her breath came out in a rush. "You believe me?"

"I don't think you'd be interested enough in history to research all this otherwise. However it is a little…

"Far-fetched?"

Crystal laughed. "You have to admit…"

"Come on. I'll show you. You'll need to change your clothes."

*　　　*　　　*　　　*　　　*

Crystal gasped when the wall of the cellar opened, but her excitement was palpable when Mattie squeezed through the doors of the chapel.

"Oh Mattie, Natalia's mirror. This is… oh I don't have the words. It's intact. This used to hang above the fireplace in the Master suites of the Manor."

"It gets better. Only you have to promise to keep it to yourself for the time being."

"Why? A find like this it's… not to mention a chapel that doesn't show on the plans of the manor at least not in the last one hundred and fifty years of bluepr…"

Crystal trailed off as Mattie touched the mirror, watched it ripple, and then passed her hand through. Her disbelief was obvious and Mattie knew she wasn't so sure she had actually seen what she thought she had. With a smile Mattie stepped into Bastian's world and turned. Oddly she couldn't see her mum or any of the chapel though she knew the mirror was directly in front of her. Stepping forward again she returned to her Mother's side.

Crystal made a strangled sound. "Wha…? You… that is… I saw…"

"You're taking it well."

"Sure." She squeaked. "Oh my… wow… I mean what… that is… how did you do that?"

"Not sure exactly, it just happened."

Stepping forward Crystal touched the glass, but for her… it was a normal mirror.

"You believe me now?"

"A little bit." Crystal teased, and Mattie wished she knew what her mother was thinking. She appeared to be taking it very well, but watching your daughter disappear through a mirror was not an everyday occurrence.

"So what do we do?" She asked.

"Firstly you need to say sorry for your recent attitude then we knuckle down to figuring out how to break this curse."

"Sorry I guess I've been a pain in the butt."

"Don't apologise to me, apologise to Bastian. When I said we, I meant the three of us."

*   *   *   *   *

The pain was so excruciating that he did not realise Matilda was there until he felt her fingers massaging his head. The twisting agony eased slowly under her manipulation but she continued even after he sighed in relief at the release from pain. Fighting the temptation to let her continue and simply bask in the feel of her tender care, he lifted his head and stood.

"Thank you." He whispered as he turned away.

There was nothing else he could say. He had condemned himself, he could not lie to her, yet he could not undo the past. For so long he'd wanted to take back his actions to save himself from the hell of this prison but now he wanted to take back his actions, to have her trust again.

"I'm sorry Bastian. I didn't want it to be true and over reacted." Stunned he turned to face her. "You've been punished enough. I see that now and I know you've changed."

He gave her a half smile. "I have changed?"

"Yeah." She closed the gap between them. "You were a womaniser... and yet, when I came into your world after so many years on your own… you didn't try anything with me. Besides if you hadn't done… well what you did, then I'd never have met you. I am sorry Bastian, please forgive me."

"We have shared a kiss." He reminded her feeling a weight lift from his shoulders.

"Yes, but that was trying to get me out of here, it wasn't anything to do with your own pleasure."

"I will not deny it was pleasurable."

He watched her blush.

"Yeah, well anyway what I guess I'm saying is…"

"Apology accepted, Matilda."

"You sure?"

"Completely."

He could not begin to describe how relieved he was. He had thought never to see her again.

"Good. I'm glad, now we can get on with getting you out of here. I hope you don't mind but I've told my Mum about you and she's going to help."

"You have told your Mother… about me?"

"Yep and she's going to help."

"I do not…"

"She's a historian. She'll be able to help you when I'm gone."

Staring at her he slowly frowned hoping he had heard incorrectly.

"Are you going somewhere?"

"I have to go home Bastian. This is my last week in England."

Her words echoed in his head as his chest constricted painfully.

"Then we had better find the answer.' He heard himself say as if from far away. He felt disconcertingly discombobulated - as though not connected to his body.

"We will."

The next few days flew past as though each hour were a minute. Each waking moment was used to franticly scramble for the missing pieces. While at night, as she slumbered, he would solidify her bed and lie beside her, simply drinking in her presence. Most of the time he worked on the breaking of the curse, but at other times he would release the research materials and simply watch her sleep. He was losing her, and there was not a thing he could do about it.

Leaning against the mirror in the dining room he watched her dine with her family. On the morrow she would be gone, flying to her home in an airplane.

"Why God?" He spoke out loud looking up to the darkness above him as he let himself fade from the mirror. "Why allow her to pass into this hell of mine, only to take her away again? I do not pretend to understand any of what has happened to me, but Matilda's presence makes the least amount of sense. I will always cherish the time we have spent together but perhaps it is too little, too late. The very notion of letting her go… hurts too much. I know I could simply hold her here with me, but as much as I wish her to stay I have no intention of condemning her. God, give me the strength and courage to do that which I need to do." Anger at the situation suddenly overwhelmed him and he slammed his fist into the nearest mirror. He was useless. There was no action he could take that would change the course of what was to come. Clenching his jaw he scrubbed his hands over his face in frustrated despair, cursing the sudden flaring of another agonizing headache. Opening his eyes again he found that once more the mirrors had closed off their view of the solid world.

"Why are you doing this to me?" He demanded into the darkness. The effort thudded through his head, magnifying the headache to such an intensity that he slid down the black mirror to the floor cradling his head in his hands. "Have I not been punished long enough?" He whispered. "I can not fight this any longer."

His mind thrust forward an image of Matilda winking at him with a smile over some jest, and he felt a tangible pain in his chest. He knew his course of action… and he was determined that it must be.

"Let it end."

Chapter Eighteen

"So I just have to know…" Jonathan began as he passed the beans along. "Since you're going home tomorrow, *did* you figure out the curse?"

Mattie speared a carrot slice with her fork. "No, unfortunately, but I do know that vanity has to do with womanising rather than looks. The Ashcombe males who cheat on their wives end up trapped behind the mirrors."

Jonathan laughed. "Just call me Alice."

"I'm not kidding."

Mattie trailed off as Tiffany's cutlery clattered suddenly against her plate.

"Sorry." Tiffany said as everyone turned to look at her. "Your idea just made me think of something."

"You can't leave us hanging now." Crystal teased.

"It's just that… never mind, it's a crazy story my family tells, when everyone has a little too much to drink."

"How is that not leaving us hanging?" Jonathan asked.

Tiffany laughed. "Fine the story goes that if our husbands did cheat on the females of the family, they had better be certain they never find out."

"Why is that?" Alex asked.

"They disappear."

Jonathan grinned. "The girls?"

"The husbands."

Mattie froze with her fork to her mouth then slowly lowered her hand.

"Probably killed them and buried them in the backyard." Jonathan laughed.

"You said the other day, your family ran alongside the Ashcombes. Any chance the husbands who supposedly disappeared were Ashcombes?" Mattie asked. Heart racing she waited for the answer barely daring to breathe. Tiffany had also said the love potion was from her family as were the Russian mirror makers.

"They could have been I suppose." Tiffany shrugged.

"Natalia comes from your family doesn't she?"

"Who's Natalia? Alex asked.

"The wife of Earnest Ashcombe back in the 1500's." Crystal explained but her attention was also on Tiffany. "I didn't know your family was Russian."

"Way back when."

"So do your family stories say more on the disappearances?"

"Just a couple of names of the guys who were supposed to have disappeared."

"Let me guess." Mattie said before she actually thought about what she was saying.

Jonathan laughed again. "You may be good at puzzles Mattie but…"

"Walter Fredrick, William Michael, Leonard Christian and Sebastian Richard. Ashcombe's all."

Tiffany stared at her. "Wow. There's only three, but you got them."

"Who'd she get wrong?" Crystal asked.

"I've never heard of Sebastian."

"He's one of my ancestors she's infatuated with." Jonathan explained, rolling his eyes as he took a sip of his wine.

Mattie shook her head in confusion. "I'm not wrong. He's one of them."

"None of my family stories mention him Mattie, but you've got to be onto something to get the others right like that." Tiffany snapped her fingers.

"Of course," realization dawned on Mattie. "In the 1800's, was anyone in your family a nanny or a nursery maid of some kind to the Cranston family?"

It was Tiffany's turn to frown. "Possibly. I don't know when it was but there is a story that one of our ancestors had a child out of wedlock and the Cranston's adopted her. The biological mother, so the story goes, gained employment with the family to have contact with her. I can't say for sure that it was in the 1800's though, it could have been early last century for all I know."

There was no doubt in Mattie's mind that the 'gypsy nanny' whom Bastian had spoken about was the biological mother, meaning Penelope was a Dolembo. From the look on her mum's face, she'd had the same thought.

"Your family is bad for the Ashcombe business." Jonathan teased. "You can look but you can't touch. Now that would be a curse."

Mattie's stomach clenched. "I think it would be worse to be trapped and watch those you loved die with age, unable to be with them."

"It would make you understand what true love was." Tiffany observed. "If you couldn't touch, you wouldn't be able to give in to your lust"

Mattie knew Tiffany spoke about herself but she felt like applauding the way she pointed it out. If Jonathan could rein in his lusts he might actually have a chance at escaping the curse.

"I don't know." Alex said as he spooned more potato onto his plate. "Asking Jonathan to give up girls might be asking a little more than he can chew."

"Is that a dare?" Jonathan grinned.

"It's a challenge." Tiffany answered softly. Mattie was surprised there was no challenge in her tone.

"I can do it. For how long, a week?"

"Two months."

"Oh come on, be reasonable."

Tiffany merely smiled and cut into her lamb.

"Fine." Jonathan muttered. "I'll do it, two months. And once I've done this I want each of you to get off my back about girls. Deal?"

Mattie held her hands in surrender. "I'm not agreeing to that. I'll be in Australia."

While the other three ribbed Jonathan about what he'd just agreed to do or, more to the point, not do, Mattie glanced at the mirror above the fireplace. As interesting as it was to have some more questions answered, and step a little closer to the riddle of how the curse began, it didn't help her get any closer to the solution of how to end it… and she was out of time.

*   *   *   *   *

He felt warm arms wrapped around his chest as Matilda embraced him from behind. He knew she would come. Thankfully the view through the windows had reappeared and his headache had waned. He could not appear weak now.

"Oh Bastian."

She held him tightly against her. Gently he turned in her arms strangely at peace with the outcome despite their failure.

"Matilda." He whispered into her hair. "I need you to make me a promise."

"What?" She asked without moving from his side.

"When you leave here, I wish for you to speak with your Mother. You are to tell her to cease the research." He said quietly and calmly.

She tensed in his arms and pulled away. "What? No, Bastian, we'll keep going, we'll figure it out."

Lifting his hand he gently ran it over her face trying to burn her features into his memory.

"With your tenacity and your Mother's knowledge, I have no doubt as to the truth of your words, but I no longer wish it." Placing his fingers over her mouth he silenced whatever she had been about to say. "I have been here for more than a century Matilda. I am older than a man ought to be. I am tired of it."

"I thought you didn't get tired."

She spoke in jest but he could hear the catch in her voice and see the tears welling in her eyes.

"I am tired of existing." The pain and grief in her expression gripped his heart as her tears broke their banks and trailed silently down her cheeks. "If I could only have met you in 1869, when it was required that I should marry. *You* are a woman of character, of intellect, of talent and honest beauty Matilda, and the need to leave you is the only regret I have in making my decision. I no longer have the desire to fight that which has has been set in motion."

"But you'll fade away. I can't let you do that Bastian."

"Do not be sad for me. I am history, and all history fades in time."

"You are not history. You are here, now. You are real, I can feel you."

"I am honoured to have met you Miss Matilda Holmes, and I will carry you here…" He placed his fingers at his temple then moved it to his heart. "…and here."

As she began to cry in earnest he drew her closer and gripped his fist behind her back. Resolved that this was the better thing, to fade in time, letting her go was still the hardest thing he ever had to do. Gradually her weeping ceased but she continued to hold fast to him as if he would disappear, as he supposed he would.

"I need for you to promise to let me go." He whispered into her hair.

"I can't." She shifted in his arms, looking up at him without pulling away. "I love you."

His breath left in a rush as he looked down at her face gazing up at him. It was extraordinarily hard not to give into temptation, but she did not wait for him to win his battle. Lifting her hand to the back of his neck she brought her own lips to his. Unable to resist her he returned the kiss pouring into it every flare of emotion in his heart. It was a kiss of bitter-sweetness.

Before his precarious hold on his self-control completely disappeared he broke the kiss and taking her hand led her to that loathsome mirror.

"Please, promise me." He said trying desperately to keep his emotions in check. He wanted nothing more than for her to stay.

She held him close for the longest time then whispered into his chest. "I promise."

Stepping back she brought her hand up to caress his face. "I won't ever forget you Bastian, I don't want to do this, but for you I will."

With her tears falling freely she again pressed her lips to his and he took her into his arms for the last time. He wanted to remember the feel of her, the taste of her, everything that was Matilda. He felt her breath in his mouth and stepped forward to bring her closer. Slowly he broke the kiss again and opened his eyes drinking in the last sight of her.

"You must leave now."

She buried her head in his chest and did not reply. Suddenly he froze as he looked up. He could see the altar… and the chapel… in fact…

"Bastian..."

Very slowly he turned. Behind him was the mirror.

"You're free."

"With single breath, mirror pass'ed be." He quoted in awesome wonder. "Thank you God. Matilda I…"

Suddenly a woman's voice echoed behind them.

"Ashcombe man in reflection thou will stay, hidden in sight thy debt to pay, Ashcombe man thy vanity keep thee, till Love shines Beauty in purity, till shattered heart within pierce free and with single breath, mirror pass'ed be."

Then with a boom the mirror behind them rippled continuously with greater and greater ferocity until it shattered abruptly and rained broken glass all around them.

They clung together under the shower and even in the moments after. They could only stare at each other, and then Matilda began to laugh, holding him close and kissing him again.

"Bastian…"

Without warning a massive headache hit him dropping him to his knees.

"Bastian what's the matter? Oh my God, no, no, no."

Looking down he saw what had Matilda so horrified. His body had begun to ripple akin to that of the glass in the mirror.

"Bastian."

He reached for her. "Mati…

Chapter Nineteen

Mattie screamed as Bastian shattered. She felt the pain as the pieces of glass tore at the skin of the arm she had raised to protect her face, but it was nothing compared to the pain ripping through her heart.

Dropping her arms she prayed he would still be there in front of her when she opened her eyes. It didn't work. He was gone. There was nothing left. Not even pieces of glass on the ground. It had all disappeared.

She had no cuts on her arms and the chapel was as it had been. The mirror was intact and showed only her own reflection.

"Bastian. No."

Mattie pressed her hand repeatedly against the glass. It stayed firm beneath her touch. It didn't ripple.

"Bastian, please."

Dropping to her knees she kept trying the glass as tears distorted the view of her own reflection.

"That's not fair Natalia. He was free. He was out of the mirror. How dare you? Give him back. I freed him. Please. I love him. Doesn't that mean anything to you?"

Mattie didn't know what she expected but the silence hurt. Natalia was long dead. She couldn't answer. All hope was lost. Bastian was gone.

The sobs tore from her and she was unable to move. She cried for so long that exhaustion wrapped itself around her and she couldn't stop shaking.

Darkness came to claim her and she didn't fight it. She didn't want to.

*   *   *   *   *

"Mattie."

Squinting Mattie rolled over and looked up as her mum came closer to the bed. "You gave us a scare sweetheart. Alex has gone to call for the Doctor."

"Doctor?"

"I found you in the chapel and you wouldn't wake up.

Mattie gasped as everything came rushing back. "He's gone Mum. I freed him, but he shattered. He's gone."

"Oh Mattie."

Crystal sat on the bed and Mattie curled into her arms like a child. She even think that she had any tears left but they still came.

"You freed him?"

Slowly Mattie told her everything, from Bastian's request that they give up trying to solve the riddle of the curse, right up to the shattering end. By the time she had finished, they were both crying.

"Oh honey. I suppose that even if he'd lived to a hundred he would have died in the thirties. Perhaps he couldn't exist outside the mirror today."

The thought only made Mattie cry harder.

"Crystal, I've… is everything okay?" Alex came into the room.

"She found out today that a friend of hers passed away. Perhaps we should cancel Doctor Miller."

"Let him come. He might give her something to help."

*   *   *   *   *

Mattie let herself be talked into staying in England longer. After a call to Clarinda to explain the situation, using the story her mum had improvised about the friend passing away, Mattie began to deal with her grief in the same way she dealt with everything.

She drew. Pages and pages. Endless images. Everything and nothing. And Bastian. Always Bastian.

Crystal happily let her spend hours at a time buried in her sketches but Alex, Jonathan and even Tiffany kept trying to interrupt.

"I beg your pardon. Are you Matilda?"

Mattie winced and turned from her drawing to face the slender elderly woman who stepped into the sunroom.

"Mattie's fine."

"How do you do? I am Tiffany's… grandmother. I own the art gallery in town. She thought you and I might have something to chat about."

It took Mattie a moment to switch her mind from 'drawing mode' to 'being sociable' mode and

176

during this time the older woman perused the sheets of paper tacked to the glass walls.

"Sorry for the mess." Mattie managed.

"Least of my worries dear."

"They're not quite finished."

"No artist ever thinks they are."

Mattie wanted to cover her unfinished drawings but somehow that felt rude. There was something about this woman's calm and casual demeanour which clashed with the intensity of her eyes. Eyes, which right now, were trained on her.

"I've got coffee if you want one. No tea though."

"Coffee would be lovely. Thank you. Black, no sugar."

Mattie was glad for the activity as she made the drinks. "What do I call you? I mean I can't call you Grandmother can I?"

"I don't mind dear, but my name is Lissie. You have quite a talent. I very nearly expect him to step from the page."

"Thank you."

"The Ashcombe family owes him a great debt."

Mattie slowly turned back to face her. "Sorry?"

"The paradox of his birth saved countless Ashcombes from the same fate."

Mattie could only stare at her.

"Come now dear. It's not as if you don't know what I speak of. You have the Ashcombe shard within your heart."

"You know about Bastian?"

"There we go, and thank you for not pretending otherwise. The kettle is boiling dear."

It took Mattie a second to notice the telling whistle, then another second to register the change of subject. Hurriedly she poured the hot water, then added milk to her own.

"Does Tiffany know?" She handed Lissie the coffee. "Did she ask you here to talk to me?"

"No dear. While I myself do not practice, the mark has been handed down generation after generation. I can feel the limbo. The curse has not quite finished with him, however it is not yet ready to accept another. Which is why this wedding is so interesting. An Ashcombe and a Dolembo who actually love each other. Perhaps this will end it after all."

"What wedding?"

Lissie looked at her for a moment before smiling. "You *have* been in the creative zone haven't you? Tiffany and Jonathan. They've been engaged for a month. They mean to marry within a few weeks. Not because she's in a family way, mind, but because she has decided that enough time has passed between them."

"She's only been waiting since she was six." Mattie mused.

"Indeed. Which is what intrigues me about you. You are not a Dolembo and yet…"

"Yet?"

"Yet, as I said before, you hold the Ashcombe shard within your heart. Only when a Dolembo loves an Ashcombe does she receive the shard. When a Dolembo is betrayed by an Ashcombe the shard shatters, and the curse is activated. You must truly love him to have received the shard."

"But he can't shatter it. He's gone."

"Tiffany says you are grieving the death of a friend, yet your drawings are of him."

"I freed him. He shattered." Mattie was surprised that she was able to say the words without crying.

"He shattered?"

"Yes." Managing to keep herself together Mattie retold what had happened. It was strange, almost like retelling the memory of a sad movie she'd seen.

"I see. Perhaps that is when…" Lissie tapped her chest over her heart. "It has happened before you realise. Not the freeing from the mirror, but a misplaced shard. As the Ashcombe curse is passed from first born to first born so too is the Dolembo curse. Except ours is through the women. Natalia was so furious that she ended up cursing her bloodline in both directions. There is only one thing that will break the curse and that is an Ashcombe living without betraying the love of a Dolembo."

"The curse isn't broken?"

"As I said before, it is in limbo. My Great-Grandmother wanted it all to end, this curse, so she stayed away from the area, drifting across Europe wherever the work would take her. Unfortunately, the child she bore was adopted by the Cranstons. The little girl grew up to become the woman he married."

"Bastian. You can say his name you know. And Penelope didn't love him. They only met once before their wedding day. Yes he betrayed her, but he couldn't possibly have betrayed her love."

"Thus the misplaced shard. Betraying the love is not necessarily betraying the person. Anichka loved Penelope and it was that love he betrayed. Until then, the assumption had been the love between a husband and wife, but it does make sense After all, not all Ashcombes have married into the Dolembo line; and Caleb, by all reports, had a blameless marriage. Yet the curse remains unbroken. To be honest, I believe the only thing to truly break the curse would be the end of either one or both of the bloodlines.

"Excuse me?" Mattie was stunned.

"It's my theory."

"Hang on a second. If your bloodline runs through Natalia, wouldn't you be of the Ashcombe bloodline?"

"Natalia was not first born. She missed out by a mere four minutes and, unfortunately for both of us, fell for a man more interested in her sister."

"Ernest loved Natalia's twin sister?" Lissie nodded and ran her fingers over the handle of the coffee cup as Mattie continued. "And he married Natalia because she was bewitching him with the Erosardoris."

Lissie nodded. "Yes."

Mattie began to pace the room as the pieces fell into place. "When the potion ceased to be effective he had an affair with the Dolembo he truly loved."

"Leaving Natalia jilted and scorned."

"Therefore she cursed both her sister…"

"The first-born of my line…"

"And her husband…"

"The first-born of the Ashcombes. Goodness now, that raises a question."

"Which is?"

"No one has had a shard since Anichka. Yours makes a strange sense. You have loved a first-born Ashcombe. Jonathan is not of the first-born line. Tiffany should not have the shard."

"Jonathan's name is on the mirror."

"Excuse me?"

"Jonathan's name is on the back of Natalia's mirror along with everyone who has ever been cursed into it."

"I do believe that Natalia is cheating."

"Natalia's dead."

"Perhaps it is time to look at the original curse." Lissie suggested.

Chapter Twenty

Normally researching the curse was something that Mattie enjoyed but as she watched her mum and Lissie go over everything yet again, then start to wade through the new diaries Lissie brought with her, she felt restless.

"Bastian said he didn't want us to continue this."

"No." Crystal lifted a finger. "He said he didn't want us to continue searching to free him. We're not doing that."

"Found it." Lissie suddenly announced pointing to a diary. "My Russian is a little rusty but… 'I can not stop the curse Natalia has cast and I can not save him, Natalia does not mean for the curse to ever be broken. She tells me if I am smart I may free Ernest from the mirror, but he will still disappear on his forty-forth birthday.' "

"She was one nasty piece of work." Crystal muttered.

"Hang on, where are you reading this from?" Mattie grabbed a seat next to Lissie.

"Olesiya's diary."

"Who's Olesiya?"

"Natalia's sister."

"The twin?"

"The very one."

"The curse can never be broken? That's not fair. Why have the riddle rhyme if there is no hope?"

"Because he can be freed from the mirror, but as I read it, it sounds like he is still cursed." Crystal answered. "On his forty-forth birthday… poof, he's gone. Sorry Mattie… I didn't mean to sound so…"

Mattie put up her hand to stop her mum from talking. "If an Ashcombe man can be freed from the mirror prior to his forty-forth birthday, why did Bastian shatter? He still had two and a half months."

Lissie continued reading. "I may not be able to remove Natalia's curse but I will counter it for further generations. My addition to her curse. If an Ashcombe man is freed from her mirror and Natalia's shard remains unshattered, than upon his cursed birthday, the love between a Dolembo and an Ashcombe will break the curse. For ever."

"Natalia's shard? What is that?" Crystal asked.

Mattie looked at Lissie, then let her explain about the metaphorical shard within both her and Tiffany's hearts.

"How can there be two? And, no offence meant, but the way Jonathan has treated Tiffany, it would have shattered by now if betrayal was the reason." Crystal tapped her pen on the table."

"She loved him despite it." Mattie pointed out.

"But yours still interests me." Lissie leaned closer to Mattie. "How can yours not be shattered when by all definitions his apparent death should have done so. Death is perhaps the biggest betrayal in love."

"I don't believe that. Anyway, it wasn't his fault. Natalia did it to him."

"But if she hadn't you wouldn't have met him."

Mattie gave a nod. That was all she could manage.

"Perhaps the limbo is Olesiya's doing. You have freed him; both you and Tiffany have unbroken shards; two of the three requirements have been fulfilled."

"The wedding." Crystal announced.

Mattie sat up straight. "The love between a Dolembo and an Ashcombe will break the curse."

"They are planning for the first of March, perhaps we can convince them to put it back a day?"

Mattie stared at her mum then at Lissie who continued. "The twenty-ninth of February. His forty-forth birthday."

"You know sweetheart, being involved with a man who is forty-four is a little hard for a mother to take."

"What?" Mattie was stunned.

"Forty-four is your greatest concern?" Lissie asked.

"Well curses and historical men are all very well and good, but forty-four is a bit much in the way of an age gap. Mattie is only twenty-eight."

"The mirror stops the aging process I believe. He was cursed in his thirty-third year."

"Thirty-three? Ok, yes, much better."

"Mum, you're crazy."

"And you're smiling. My job here is done."

*   *   *   *   *

"I've got popcorn and marshmallows, but I want all the pink ones."

Mattie glanced up as her mother came around the mirror and joined her at the altar. "Mum, what are you doing here?"

"Well it is the twenty-eighth of February, we've got an hour until midnight. I thought you'd like some company."

"Of course you knew I'd be here."

"Where else would you be?"

Mattie took the confectionery as Crystal sat down beside her. "Did you get a large coke and a movie pass while you were at it?"

"Oh ha ha."

"What did you tell Alex?"

"That you were going through some girly stuff and I was going to play Mum."

"Thanks a lot."

"What would you rather I said. You were waiting for a cursed man to appear and I thought I'd keep you company?"

"You've got a point."

"How are you holding up?"

"Okay, I guess."

"Do you want to talk about it?"

"There isn't much more to talk about. Either we've found the answer and he'll show up, or we haven't and he won't."

"Seriously Mattie, you're that calm about it? I'm near on jumping out of my skin here, and you're all c'est la vie."

To be honest with herself, Mattie knew she had been feeling strangely serene about Bastian since the moment she'd met Lissie.

"Talking about that… Mum what do you make of Lissie?"

Crystal shrugged as she popped a marshmallow into her mouth. "She seems nice enough."

"You don't think it's weird that suddenly she has all these diaries that no one has ever heard of, and knew exactly which one to go to for the apparent solution to the curse."

"I think it was a stroke of good luck, and goodness knows it's what you need right now."

"So you believe it's true?"

"Who are you and where is the real Mattie?"

"What?"

"Do I believe? Did you or did you not walk directly through that mirror right there? Did you or did you not hook up with a guy who was born in eighteen-thirty-six? And you ask if I believe?"

"It's just that it all feels not quite right. When I first met her she realised immediately that I knew about Bastian, and the curse, and her family history."

"Perhaps Tiffany told her."

"I didn't tell anyone except you about Bastian."

"But we've all spoken about the curse. Come on, we'll find out soon enough if she's right or wrong, but I, for one, am really looking forward to meeting your Bastian."

"What if you're right? What if he can't exist outside the mirror in our time. What if he ages and becomes dust."

"Are you trying to make yourself miserable?"

Mattie sucked the salt from her thumb then slowly chewed the popcorn. "I saw him shatter Mum; I'm scared it'll happen all over again."

Her mother wrapped an arm around her and Mattie watched the second hand on her watch seeming to crawl as it ticked away the time. They talked about mere day to day incidents, but fell silent when midnight came… and went. Neither of them moved. They waited. And waited. By two o'clock, Mattie had to admit the truth. Lissie's theory had been wrong. Bastian wasn't about to appear. It really was over.

Chapter Twenty-One

It was very nearly the hardest thing Mattie ever had to do in her life. She was truly happy for Tiffany and Jonathan, but she could barely manage to dredge up a smile for the happy couple. Not to mention that she was trussed up in a period style dress – corset and all.

Not many people made their guests come in fancy dress at a wedding, but Tiffany had insisted. She had even gone to the lengths of arranging for extra outfits to be on hand in case anyone tried to sneak in too modernly attired.

Admittedly the style looked stunning on Mattie, but it was near suffocating, and every time she saw herself she wanted to imagine Bastian at her side. He would have fit in perfectly here. No one would have been able to tell the difference. She only hoped that people didn't notice how she tried to avoid all possible mirrors.

"Wish me luck." Tiffany demanded as she swished for the last time in front of her mirror.

"Good luck." Mattie automatically parroted.

"Isn't this so exciting? Finally I'm here. I'm about to become Mrs Jonathan Ashcombe. Mind you with all the near catastrophes I wasn't sure I'd make it."

"Sure you would have. There's a court house in London you could elope to."

Tiffany laughed and gave Mattie a hug. "You are such a giggle. Wish me luck."

"I already have. How much of it do you think you need?"

"All I can get. With the church double booking us on tomorrow's date and needing to reschedule for today; having to hold the reception at Ashcombe Manor because the Gershim was flooded… you'd think I'd had enough bad luck wouldn't you?"

"It all turned out well enough."

"Yes it did, wonderfully well indeed. Oh, there's Daddy, I have to go. Wish me…"

"Yes, I know. Good luck."

Mattie made her way down to the foyer entry with the others. Amazingly it wasn't a tight squeeze, even with all the huge dresses, and when the music began they all managed to make it without tripping on each other's skirts.

The ceremony went on forever. With robed priests; songs in Latin; golden gongs and incense burners the Catholics really knew how to turn on a fanfare. Seemingly, short and sweet were words which simply had no place their vocabularies.

"I now pronounce you man and wife."

Finally it was over. All Mattie had to do now was to be sociable for the next few hours, then she could book her flight home and try to live with the knowledge that she hadn't been smart enough or good enough to save Bastian.

It was quite easy… to hide in a crowd. Apart from her mother, Alex, Jonathan or Tiffany she didn't know anyone all that well. The rest were either total strangers or only vague acquaintances.

"What are you standing here for dear? You should be out there doing what young people do. Dancing and having fun."

Mattie jumped, startled by Lissie's sudden appearance. Since she herself was standing between a brick wall and a heavy pot containing a tree, she shouldn't have missed Lissie's approach.

"It didn't work." Mattie blurted. "He didn't appear. You were wrong."

"Was I? Perhaps you were merely impatient."

"Impatient?"

"Yes. Believing it is as you say, and that he didn't appear, then I don't suppose you'd be interested in making the acquaintance of that gentleman."

"Which gentleman?" Mattie's stomach jumped so much that it seemed to strike her heart and the beat quickened as her eyes followed Lissie's gaze. The mirror Jonathan had given Tiffany was set against the wall across the stone portico and in its reflection stood… Bastian.

Numbly Mattie stumbled towards it. It couldn't be. Surely he couldn't be trapped. Not still. Not again. She stopped walking and her heart raced as she saw that her own reflection had blocked him from sight.

Slowly Mattie turned.

Bastian was right there in front of her.

All sound and movement faded away as her feet took her nearer to what her mind couldn't seem to comprehend.

"Bastian."

"Matilda." As she watched, he suddenly stumbled against a table which stood between them.

"Ouch. I need to remember that objects are constantly solid here."

Mattie half laughed, half sobbed as she realised he was truly freed and in her world this time. She almost flew around the table to greet him. Finally she was truly able to be in his arms, and she welcomed his kiss.

"Bastian." He was solid, he wasn't transparent and she couldn't stop touching him. "What happened. I saw you shatter."

"Shatter?"

"Like glass, you shattered then disappeared."

"It was you who disappeared. I reached for you one moment and the next you had gone. I called your name and it was an elderly lady who answered. She led me here to find you."

"Lissie." Mattie turned but Lissie wasn't there. In her place stood a young woman wearing a dress that seemed to have exchanged the garishness of a costume for a classical creation of period reality. Smiling she held out her hand and a handsome man stepped from nowhere to take it.

"Ashcombe man, thy curse is broken. Love well."

Before their eyes, the young woman and gentleman slowly faded from sight. Mattie's jaw dropped and she blinked several times. "Did you just see…"

"That could not have been Natalia." Bastian whispered.

"Actually it might… have been Olesiya… and maybe Ernest."

"I beg your pardon?"

"Olesiya, Natalia's twin sister."

"Perhaps you should start at the beginning."

"It's kind of a long story."

"I have no plans to leave. However I must ask about your clothing. While you are beautiful to behold, Matilda, this does not appear to be the fashionable garb for this time."

"No, it's for Jonathan and Tiffany's wedding."

"They are married?"

"About an hour ago. A Dolembo and an Ashcombe. It's what broke the curse."

"I believe you were to start at the beginning."

Mattie leaned into him again and looked up into his iridescent green eyes. "Can we leave the facts for a moment? Leave all the curses and ghosts and mirrors for another time. And just…"

Bastian pressed his lips against hers and for now, that was all the communication Mattie wanted.

THE END

www.ingramcontent.com/pod-product-compliance
Lightning Source LLC
Chambersburg PA
CBHW021017120726
47905CB00009B/3051